# UNWANTED INHERITANCE

# UNWANTED INHERITANCE

•

## Glen Ebisch

*AVALON BOOKS*
NEW YORK

PRINTED IN THE UNITED STATES OF AMERICA
ON ACID-FREE PAPER
BY HADDON CRAFTSMEN, BLOOMSBURG, PENNSYLVANIA

To my wife

## Chapter One

"So this is the Compton House," Abby said, pulling the van to a stop at the far end of the circular driveway.

"If you can call it a house. I'd say it's more like a mansion," said Heather.

The building was spread out before them at the far end of the circle: a three-story structure made of massive blocks of red stone, flanked by two wings of the same height constructed of a lighter-tan stone in smaller brick-sized shapes. Each wing was topped by medieval looking turrets.

"Are you sure that people actually live there? It looks more like a museum or a school," Abby said.

Heather agreed. Her father taught at Amherst College, and this appeared for all the world like a building lifted directly from the campus.

"The woman that I talked to on the phone said that she lived there."

"But her name was Webster, not Compton, right?" asked Abby.

"She said her uncle had left the house to her, so I guess Webster is her married name."

"And she wants us to paint a room for her?"

"She's interviewing us to see if we'd be acceptable to paint a room for her," Heather corrected.

"Well, *excuse* me," Abby said. She studied the building. "The rooms in there must be gargantuan. Just for being so uppity, I'm going to tell her she'll have to pay by the square foot."

Heather gave Abby a sharp glance.

"Promise me that you won't make any jokes. This woman sounded very stuffy, and you know . . ." she let the sentence trail off and sat there looking anxious.

Abby smiled. "I know. We need the work. Don't worry, I'll behave myself, more or less."

Heather sighed softly. Abby meant well, but her tongue often got ahead of her brain. Passionate Painters, the company she and Abby had started a little over a year ago, was surviving largely because of a booming housing market and their willingness to stand by their motto that no job was too small. A showcase job like this one, however, might be enough to get them established as the premier decorative painters in western Massachusetts. Heather didn't want to see it jeopardized by a careless comment.

They drove the rest of the way around the circle and parked in front of the massive recessed entrance with an arched overhang. Even though it was a sunny morning, the front door was shrouded in shadows.

Abby shivered as she got out of the van. "The place doesn't exactly give a sense of domestic warmth, does it? Looks like the opening scene in one of those gothic horror movies where the new bride arrives at her husband's ancestral home, little suspecting that his past three wives are buried in the wine cellar."

Heather shot her a warning look.

"Okay, okay. The gothic look can have its own appeal. When did you say it was built?"

Heather always made a point of doing background research when working on an historic home. Many owners wanted their houses decorated in a style authentic to the time when they were built.

"The woman I spoke to at the library said the center part of the house was constructed in the 1850s by Alexander Compton. He owned the big paper mill that the town grew up around. That's why the town is named Compton. The family has lived here since then, adding on the east then the west wings in the 1870s and 1890s when they needed the space and had the money. In the late 1960s the mill closed, and I guess the town pretty much went downhill after that. Most of the people who still live around here commute to jobs in Springfield or Pittsfield."

"But the house stayed in the family?"

"The librarian said that Leo Compton lived here for the last thirty years. He died six months ago, and she didn't know what was going to happen to the house now."

"Well, let's find out," Abby said.

They walked up to the front door, and Abby located the button for the bell which was inside the open mouth of a gargoyle. She gave it a long push and pretended that it had bitten her finger until Heather frowned. Abby shrugged, then gave her friend an innocent smile.

They listened but couldn't tell whether anything had sounded inside the house or not. Abby was about to let one of the lion's head door knockers do its job when the right side of the massive double doors opened. A woman in her mid-twenties wearing a white blouse and black skirt appeared.

"Are you Mrs. Webster?" Heather asked.

The woman raised one eyebrow. "I am Anna, the maid. Do you wish to see Mrs. Webster?"

No, we're just doing a door-to-door survey to see who's home in the neighborhood, Abby wanted to say. Heather somehow read her mind and gave her a silencing glance.

"Yes. We have an appointment," Heather replied. "We're the painters."

The woman frowned. "Follow me," she said, backing out of the doorway and immediately disappearing into the darkness.

After blinking several times in order to get accustomed to the sudden shadows, the women found themselves in a large entry hall. To the left and directly in front of them were sweeping staircases that went up to the second floor. A large chandelier hung from the ceiling two floors above their heads.

"Wow!" Heather said softly.

"Not your standard tract home," Abby said, pausing to study the painting technique on the walls.

Heather pulled on her arm. "The maid went that way," she said, pointing down a wide hall to the left.

"Yeah. We'd better not lose her or they'll have to call in the bloodhounds to track us."

They walked quickly down the hall, reaching the room at the end just as the maid was about to close the door in their faces. Abby shoved hard on the door before it could shut. The maid turned and glared at them as they crowded in behind her.

"The painters are here, Mrs. Webster," the maid announced, making it sound as if the neighborhood would never be the same again.

The room was at least fifty feet long, running from the front to the back of the house. The bay window at the front end told Heather that they were under one of the tower wings. At the back of the house was a set of three large casement windows that looked out on a mass of trees and shrubs.

"Thank you, Anna," a woman's voice replied from the far end of the room.

The woman who spoke had the windows at her back, so the light made her impossible to distinguish as she walked towards them. Heather wondered what she would think of them: two women in their late twenties in paint-stained jeans and denim shirts. Herself tall and willowy; Abby shorter and more full-figured.

"Well, at least you aren't little men with dirty hands," Mrs. Webster said, coming closer.

"We try not to be," Abby snapped. She felt Heather's elbow poke into her side.

As the woman drew closer, Heather could see that she was somewhere in her middle thirties. She was extremely thin. Her face had a drawn, tired look. She wore a burgundy cashmere jacket over designer jeans and a white turtleneck.

"I'm Heather Martinson and this is my partner, Abby Sinclair," Heather said, putting out her hand.

Mrs. Webster stared hard at their blue work shirts and spattered pants, then paused for an instant as if considering whether she wanted to touch the hand of a painter. Finally she took Heather's hand gingerly and held it for a moment with two fingers.

"I'm Caroline Webster."

Before she could draw her hand back, Abby reached out and seized it firmly in her own, giving it a vigorous shake. The woman grimaced and quickly pulled her hand back, holding it stiffly at her side.

"So, is this the room you want painted?" Abby asked, dodging the crystal chandelier hanging down in the center of the room, as she walked into the middle of the space and looked around.

"Yes. This is the dining room."

"Looks like someone already started on the job," said Abby. Three of the walls were a faded peach color that appeared to go back a number of decades, but the fourth wall was half covered with a fresh coat of light blue paint.

"My uncle had the furniture cleared out of the room and began to paint it himself about six months ago. But the job proved to be too much for him."

"Six months ago," said Heather. "Isn't that when . . ." she paused, not sure whether to reveal her research into the family history.

"He died." Mrs. Webster said with a complacent smile, as if she expected every workman to be familiar with her family history. "He was found at the foot of his ladder over by the blue wall. Apparently he had a heart attack and fell. Why a man over eighty would be doing work like that is beyond me."

"Lots of men in their eighties are pretty vigorous," said Abby, walking over to inspect the blue wall.

"My Uncle Leo was not. He had high blood pressure, a weak heart, and was legally blind. Painting this room was a foolish thing for him to undertake. He was simply trying to save money."

Abby appeared ready to say something in response to

that, so Heather interrupted. "What color did you have in mind for this room?"

Mrs. Webster reached into the pocket of her jacket and extracted an envelope. She carefully removed a swatch of fabric that she handed to Heather.

"I'd like you to match this."

Heather studied the deep green fabric, then handed it to Abby.

"With computers you can get paint mixed to any color you want, but why this?" Abby asked.

"You don't approve?"

"It's just that an entire room might be a bit . . . over-whelming," Heather said before Abby could express her opinion.

"This is the color of my favorite dress, and it's the color that I wish to have this room painted," Mrs. Webster said, snatching back the piece of fabric. "If that's beyond you, perhaps I should look for other painters."

"Perhaps you should," said Abby. "Our reputation depends on our work, and if we do a room the color of green algae, everyone is going to feel like they're dining on the bottom of the sea."

The woman blushed. "I'm sure I can find another painter who will see things differently."

Heather was searching for a way to smooth things over when a man spoke from the doorway.

"What color would you paint this room?" he asked, staring at Heather.

He was in his early forties, wearing a gray business suit. He smiled encouragingly at Heather to show that his question was meant in earnest.

"I think Uncle Leo was on the right track," Heather replied. "I'd go with a slightly darker blue than his, but otherwise blue is fine."

She took a quick glance at Abby, who nodded her agreement.

"I think I agree," the man said.

"George, this is my house," Caroline Webster said.

"Of course it is, my dear. But this young woman is correct, that shade of green is not appropriate for this room."

For a moment Heather thought that the woman was going to storm out. Instead she took a deep breath and nodded briefly.

"Blue will be acceptable, but I want a stenciled border along the top. Is that something you are capable of doing?"

"Of course."

"I want you to begin by Friday of this week."

"Well, we are kind of busy . . ." Abby began.

"But we'll find a way to fit you in," Heather added quickly.

"Good. On Friday morning bring some samples of stencil patterns and the colors you plan to use for me to examine," the woman said coldly. "If I approve, you can begin work." She turned without saying good-bye and walked back to the far end of the room.

"Fine. That's all set then," the man said happily. "Let me show you the way out."

Once they were out in the hall, he put out his hand to Heather and Abby.

"I'm George Webster."

"Are you her husband?" Abby asked in a tone that suggested condolences.

"Yes." He smiled as if he could appreciate the difficulty they'd been put through. "Caroline can be a little difficult at times, particularly with regard to this house. But her bark is worse than her bite. And I'm sure that once she sees the house coming along, her mood will improve."

"Have you been living here long?" asked Heather.

"I don't really live here at all. I'm staying at our apartment in Boston where my business is located. I'll come out as often as possible, of course, to keep Caroline company, but Caroline is living here alone. Her brother will be moving in this week to stay with her for the summer."

"I don't understand. Why are you fixing the house up if you aren't going to live here?" asked Abby.

"Caroline's uncle, Leo Compton, stipulated in his will that any relative who wanted to inherit a portion of the house and grounds would have to live in the house for at least three months. Caroline likes the house and wishes to own it. Fortunately, the will leaves me free to come and go as I please."

"You don't like the house?" Heather asked.

By now they were standing outside by the driveway. A silver Mercedes was parked behind their van. A young man in jeans and a blue work shirt handed Mr. Webster the keys and received a "thank you, Jack" in response.

Webster turned and looked up at the house that seemed to hang over them like a forbidding mountain cliff.

"I don't know whether I dislike this house in particular, Ms. Martinson, or whether all houses this old and filled with history make me a bit uncomfortable."

"Why is that?" Heather asked.

He shrugged. "What is history but the diary of people's triumphs and failures? This house has seen a lot of that. It's in the air. You can smell it."

"That's just mildew," said Abby.

Mr. Webster laughed. "Well, whatever it is, I prefer

places that are new and shiny and contemporary. The more glass and chrome the better."

He walked around to the driver's side of the Mercedes, then turned back.

"But I am looking forward to seeing what you can do to the old place. Maybe a couple of young people like yourselves will be able to drive out some of the dismal old spirits. Can you give me a rough estimate of what the job in the dining room will cost?"

Heather and Abby glanced at each other, then Heather named a figure.

"But that's only an estimate. It could be a bit more or less."

"In my experience it's never less, although in your case I may be wrong," said Mr. Webster with a smile. "I'll have a check for half that amount waiting for you on Friday. Happy painting!"

With a wave he got in the car and drove away.

"Seems like a nice guy," said Heather.

"He'd be a wet blanket at a party," Abby observed, as they headed back to the van. "All that talk about history and spirits. You'd think he was trying to tell us the place is haunted."

Heather remained silent.

Abby looked over at her. "You don't believe that sort of nonsense, do you? I'd hate to think that I had a partner who spent her spare time talking to ghosts."

"I don't believe in ghosts," Heather said with a smile. "But I do think places take on a kind of atmosphere because of the things that have happened there."

Abby gave her an 'Oh, spare me' look.

They pulled around the circular drive and headed back to the main road.

"Do you think Mr. Webster was right about his wife's bark being worse than her bite?" Heather asked.

Abby snorted. "I'd say that if Caroline Webster took a bite out of you, you'd need a rabies shot pretty quick."

Heather grinned at her friend. "I wouldn't have put it so colorfully, but I'm afraid that I agree with you."

As they pulled through the gate and stopped before heading onto the main road, a car slowed and turned into the driveway. Heather glanced down as the car passed. The man behind the wheel looked up at exactly the same time, and their eyes met. He smiled quickly, then he was gone. Although Heather couldn't have explained how or why the moment took her breath away.

"You can go now," Abby said, oblivious to what had happened.

"Right," Heather mumbled, wondering if she'd ever see him again.

## Chapter Two

"How ironic," Heather's mother exclaimed so loudly that Heather held the phone away from her ear.

"What's ironic?" Heather asked. She had just finished telling her mother about her visit to the Compton House and Mrs. Webster's reluctant job offer.

"Well, over thirty years ago, when I was just starting out, it was a commission from the Comptons that got my career going. The three brothers, Leo, Anthony and Alex, had me paint a group portrait of them. They wanted something to put over the mantel in the wretched drawing room of their great drafty castle."

"How come you never told me about it?"

Her mother hesitated. "To be honest, it wasn't one of my successes. I don't think they liked the final result very much. Actually, I believe that Leo and Anthony were satisfied enough, but Alex, he was the youngest, made a terrible fuss. He always struck me as a sly little man and I'm afraid . . . well, you know."

Heather well knew that her mother valued honesty above all in her art. She'd made a successful career out of painting the rich and famous, not because she flattered them, but because she showed them as they actually were. Surprisingly few famous people were bothered by being portrayed with unvarnished realism, warts and all.

"So the end result didn't make Alex happy?" asked Heather.

"They paid me, but I believe Alex objected to having the picture put on display. I have no idea where it is now. Leo inherited the house a few years later, after their father Reginald died. He probably stuck the painting up in one of those dark hallways. Fortunately, the middle brother Anthony was particularly taken with my work and his early recommendations to several friends in Boston proved very helpful."

Heather pulled the notes she had taken in the library about the Compton family across her desk and scanned them.

"Anthony would be the father of Caroline, the woman who's hiring me."

"That's right. When I painted the picture she was a small child of maybe two or three, and her father doted on her," Heather's mother said in a faraway voice. "That's all I remember. I believe a boy was born a few years later, but I never met him."

"Well, Caroline has become quite a woman," said Heather. She went on to give an abbreviated version of their meeting.

Heather's mother gave a throaty chuckle. "I've warned you before, the worst people to work for are the ones who didn't earn their money but had it handed to them. They spend the rest of their lives trying to prove that ancestry is as important as accomplishment."

"I'll just flatter her and stay out of her way."

"What about Abby? She's not very good at that."

"I guess I'll have to put a muzzle on her. At least George Webster seemed like a reasonable guy, and he's the one who's paying the bills."

"But he won't be there every day."

"Are you saying that I shouldn't take the job?" Heather asked.

She guessed that her mother's lack of enthusiasm was mostly due to her long-standing regrets at having a daughter who had majored in studio art, and had shown some talent as an artist, 'wasting herself' as a decorative painter.

"Of course not, this is a wonderful opportunity. Just remember to be careful to get some money up front and have them keep paying as you go along. That way, if they don't like the final result, you'll still have your money. The rich can be the worst ones at paying bills. They think you should be grateful to work for them."

"I'll remember."

"When do you start?"

"Tomorrow morning I'm going to show my samples to Mrs. Webster. Abby is finishing up another job, but if Mrs. Webster approves of my choices, we should both be over there working in the afternoon."

"I hope you're successful in brightening the place up a bit. When I think back to the time I spent there while having the brothers sit for me, all I can remember are all the shadows."

Heather smiled at her mother's way of remembering everything in terms of light and dark.

"It is kind of a gloomy place."

"Hmm. Somehow it seemed to be more than that. You know, what Alex didn't like about my painting was that he seemed to almost disappear into the shadows beside the fireplace. He insisted that it hadn't actually been very dark in that part of the room. He was correct, of course, but at the time I couldn't very well tell him the truth."

"Which was?"

"That the darkness was coming from inside of him."

"Your mother is scary sometimes," Abby said the next morning, as she helped Heather load the ladder into the van.

Heather was getting ready to go to the Compton House, while Abby was planning to return to finish up a job at a local restaurant.

"She doesn't mean to be," Heather said, "but she gets these impressions of people."

"If you're talking about auras, I'm going to leave."

Heather smiled. "Mom isn't any more New Age than you are. She would just say that if you look at people with an artistic sensitivity, you can tell things about their character."

"Still sounds too far out to me," Abby replied, shoving some paint buckets and a tarp in next to the ladder. "Anyway, this Alex guy isn't at the house, is he?"

"George Webster didn't mention him, and I don't see how Anthony's children would be the only ones in line to inherit the house if Alex was still alive. He was the youngest of the brothers."

Abby shrugged. "Don't worry about it. You've got enough to think about with the taste-impaired Mrs. Webster hanging around. I'll come over as soon as I can to provide some assistance."

Heather rolled her eyes. "That should be enough to get us both fired."

"You underestimate my diplomatic skills," Abby said, getting into her car. "Ten minutes of my charming personality and Caroline Webster will be eating out of my hand."

"Like the last time, when she was ready to fire us before we even had the job."

Abby waved airily out the car window. "An aberration. Her ugly green dress took me by surprise. Don't worry. I'll be on my best behavior starting today."

"I'll be depending on that."

After Abby had driven off to finish their job in the restaurant, Heather closed up the van and slowly drove out to the Compton House. Pushed to its limit, the old van could probably make the trip in half an hour, but Heather got there forty minutes later, having taken her time on the sunny spring day. Even though it was late April, spring was only just arriving on the eastern side of the Berkshires. The ground had dried out from the snowmelt and leaves were starting to unfold, finally convinced that they wouldn't be cut down by a late winter storm.

Heather also had not rushed because she doubted that Mrs. Webster was the kind of woman who would want to be disturbed by painters before nine o'clock. When she arrived, Heather discovered that she needn't have delayed.

"Go right to work," Anna, the maid, said, waving down the hall toward the dining room with an imperious gesture worthy of her employer.

"But Mrs. Webster wanted to approve the colors and talk about stencils before I began work."

Anna shrugged. "Mrs. Webster said that if she

couldn't have the room painted her favorite shade of green, why should she care what color it is?" The maid pulled a check out of her apron pocket and pushed it toward Heather. "Mr. Webster left this for you."

Heather took the check and before she could think of a response, the maid had turned and disappeared through a door that led into the back of the house.

Fortunately all the priming materials that she needed to start painting were already loaded on the van, so Heather went back out and took out her ladders, tarps, paint, buckets, and brushes. She arranged everything next to the door. Then, holding the door open with her hip, she began wrestling the first of her two twelve-foot wooden ladders into the lobby.

"Let me help," someone said from behind her, and the ladder suddenly lifted up. As Heather held the door, the young man she had seen give George Webster his keys the other day carried the ladder into the lobby. "Thanks," she said as he carefully placed the ladder against the wall.

When he turned toward her and smiled, she could see that he was even younger than she had guessed the other day, no more than nineteen or twenty.

"I'm Jack," he said, sticking out his hand.

Heather introduced herself.

"What do you do around here?" she asked.

"Pretty much whatever anyone wants me to do. Technically I'm the assistant gardener, but just about anyone can boss me around. I'm kind of at the bottom of the food chain."

"Have you worked here long?"

"About a year. Leo Compton hired me about six months before . . . you know."

"Before he died."

"Yeah. It's not such a bad deal, actually. I go to the community college part time. They let me live here over the old stable, and I can eat in the kitchen." He came closer and lowered his voice. "The pay is pretty good, and Lloyd, he's the gardener, isn't so bad, at least not if you don't mind being bossed around by someone who reminds you of your grandfather."

"Sometimes you have to put up with people in order to earn money," Heather said, thinking of her own position.

"That's the truth," said Jack. "How about I help bring your stuff down to the dining room?"

Heather happily agreed, and between the two of them they had all of her gear safely in the dining room within ten minutes. He was helping her spread the canvas tarp along the end of the room where she was going to begin when they were interrupted.

"Boy, what are you doing in here?"

Heather turned and saw an elderly man in a flannel shirt and blue overalls standing in the doorway. Most of his face was covered in a scraggly white beard.

"Just helping the painter, Lloyd."

Lloyd looked Heather over slowly and licked his lips. "Well, boy, I can see why you might rather work with her than with me. At your age I'd have felt the same way. But you're a field hand, not a house servant, and I've got a row that needs to be dug for some hedges. Maybe you can come back and check on the little lady after we're done, if you've still got any energy left, that is."

He turned and disappeared through the doorway.

"Sorry, I'd better go," Jack said. "Lloyd doesn't like to have to ask twice."

"Does he really remind you of your grandfather?"

Heather asked, wondering what kind of family Jack came from.

Jack laughed. "He isn't so bad. He just likes to act grumpy, that's all."

Giving Heather a wave and promising to check back later, Jack left.

Suddenly aware that this was the first time she'd been alone in the dining room, Heather did a pirouette, trying to take it all in. She had to admit that George Webster was right, there was a certain strange quality about the place.

Heather thought the lived-in look that made Mr. Webster find the house oppressive was a link to the history of the place. It was fine to make changes and redecorate, but it should always be done so as to preserve the beauty of what had been created in the past.

No perfect stainless steel and glass for me, Heather decided, as she carried her step ladder across the room. They'll look pretty much the same fifty years from now as they do today. I want materials that will change and mature with time right along with the people living there.

Heather spread a canvas tarp over the oak floor, which she noted was also in need of sanding and refinishing. Then she set up her ladder in front of the wall that Leo Compton had been working on when he died. He had been putting his robin's egg blue paint right over the peach color of decades before, and some of the pink color had bled through. That made clear what she had already guessed: the entire room would need a coat of white primer before putting on the new shade of blue that she had in mind.

Heather carried over a gallon of the primer, pried it open, and after stirring it thoroughly, poured some in her cardboard painter's bucket. Carefully balancing the bucket and her trim brush, she climbed to the top of her twelve-foot ladder. She would first need to prime by brush under the wide crown molding, before covering space more quickly using a roller. As frequently happened on the job, Heather found herself being thankful for her height of almost five-ten. It may have made me feel conspicuous and gawky in high school, she thought, but when you have fifteen-foot ceilings and a twelve-foot ladder every extra inch of reach helps.

She would paint along the molding as far as she could safely reach, before coming down and moving the ladder. Going up and down the ladder was tiring but essential, and good knees were as important as good taste in being a decorative painter. As she began to work, Heather soon developed a rhythm and drifted off in a world of her own, imagining a bright future for Passionate Painters.

She had just reached the corner and was ready to get her roller and tray when she heard a sound at the foot of the ladder. She looked down and saw a man staring up at her. The man she had seen in the car yesterday.

"Can I help you?" she asked, taking refuge in formality from her surprise and nervousness.

His face broke into a wide smile. "Sorry if I startled you, but the way you were standing there reminded me of something."

"What?" Heather asked.

"I'm not sure. Possibly a statue of Diana, the Greek goddess of the hunt."

"I'd have to be a Roman copy or else I'd be missing some important body parts. There aren't any Greek ones that are still whole."

His eyes opened wide in surprise.

"But right now," Heather continued, "I feel more like 'Galatea' by Raphael."

He looked puzzled for a moment, then laughed. "The beautiful nymph pursued by the ugly Cyclops?"

"Exactly."

Why did I say that? Heather thought. Here's a guy I like on first sight and already I'm insulting him. But that little art reference he'd thrown in to prove how smart he was annoyed her. She hadn't liked it when guys did it in college to show off, and she'd liked it even less in the artists she'd later dated.

"Look, I apologize. What I said did sound like an incredibly pompous pick-up line," he said in a contrite voice. "But couldn't you come down from the ladder? I'm getting a stiff neck looking up at you, and I'd really like to say I'm sorry face to face."

"I'm done up here anyway," Heather admitted grudgingly and came down the ladder.

When she reached the floor, Heather took her time setting down her bucket and brush before straightening and turning toward the man. He was taller than her skewed view from the ladder had led her to believe, at least three inches taller than herself, and she had to tilt her head up slightly to look into his face.

"That's better, isn't it?" he said, and smiled.

Her gaze started with his white teeth, traveled to his deep brown eyes, then moved along his wide forehead to the light-brown hair that went down to curl at the collar of his slightly dirty blue work shirt. Then her eyes traveled over the wide shoulders, across his broad chest, to his trim hips in tight scruffy jeans. She noted his strong hands with their long tapered fingers. Late twenties and no wedding ring, she thought, and was immediately annoyed with herself for noticing.

Her eyes returned to his, and she saw he was taking in her examination of him with amusement.

"Sorry, it's the painter in me," she mumbled.

"I hope you liked what you saw," he said, then waved a hand indicating that she should ignore that remark. "There I go again sounding like a cheap lounge lizard."

Heather stuck out her hand. "I'm Heather Martinson. As you can see I'm a painter. Are you another gardener?"

The man appeared confused but took her hand.

"Why do you say that?"

"Well, I've met two gardeners already this morning," she explained. "I thought that maybe you might be another."

"Probably my clothes fooled you. I was just moving in and didn't want to worry about being neat."

"Moving in? Then you must be Mrs. Webster's brother."

"That's right. I'm Michael Compton," he said.

Heather gently wiggled her hand to indicate that he could release it, which he did reluctantly.

"You said that you're a painter," Michael said. "You didn't mean just doing this."

"I don't *just* do this," Heather said, "This is what I do."

"Well, what I meant was that your average painter of walls wouldn't know about Greek sculpture or Galatea. And she wouldn't have given me such a professional once-over."

"You'd be surprised what your average *painter of walls*, as you put it, knows," Heather said, abruptly squatting down to clean her brush in a jar of water.

Hearing a sigh, she glanced up. Michael Compton was

looking at her with a mixture of exasperation and amusement.

"Look, it seems that I'm doomed to spend the rest of my days starting over with you. I repeatedly say the wrong thing or else you take it the wrong way. Can we call a truce?" He reached down. She grabbed his hand, and he easily pulled her to her feet.

She smiled guiltily. "Okay, maybe I did overreact. But people are always saying that just because I have a fine arts degree I shouldn't be wasting my time painting walls."

"Some of the greatest artists in the Renaissance painted walls," he replied.

Heather laughed. "I'm not exactly doing frescoes here. Now how is it that you know so much about art?"

"Like you, I majored in art, but I specialized in the history of art. I went on to grad school, and I'm sort of a curator at the Boston Museum of Fine Arts."

"Sort of?"

He looked away as if embarrassed.

"I'm on a leave of absence for the summer. I thought I'd help Caroline move in here and stay with her for a few months."

"That's very nice of you. I'm sure that moving here after living in Boston will be a difficult adjustment for her."

Michael nodded. "So what do you think of the house?" he asked.

"I've only just arrived, but it certainly has character to spare. Have you spent much time here?"

"When I was a child, my parents used to bring Caroline and me here on holidays to visit Uncle Leo. He never married and had no children of his own, so I think my parents figured that he'd like to see us. We'd run all over and have a wonderful time. Although I have to admit, we usually stayed together."

"Afraid of getting lost?" Heather asked.

"No, we pretty much knew our way around." He paused, considering the question. "For years Uncle lived here alone except for an old couple, the Baxters. Mrs. Baxter cooked and her husband was kind of a butler. A woman from town would come up during the day to clean. So all in all, the house was pretty empty. I think it was the emptiness of it all that kind of spooked us. When my father was a boy living here with his parents and two brothers the place was usually filled with people, but after my grandfather died and Uncle Leo took over, I guess it became a different kind of place, more depressing."

"Maybe houses get lonely, too," Heather said.

"Sometimes it certainly feels that way," he said, glancing around the dining room.

"The Baxters aren't here any more?"

Michael shook his head. "They both died. He died some years ago, but his wife continued cooking for Uncle Leo until she passed away about three years ago. That's when he hired the new cook, Mrs. Maxwell."

"And all the gardeners," Heather said with a teasing grin.

Michael smiled. "Lloyd has been coming up from town for years to putter around on the grounds. I'm not sure how much he actually accomplishes, but he and Uncle Leo had a symbiotic relationship: Lloyd would work for low wages and my uncle wasn't known for being generous."

"What about Jack?"

"I didn't even know about him until Uncle Leo died. It was at my uncle's funeral that I found out that Jack had been living above the old stables for six months. I'm a little ashamed to admit it, but I hadn't been out here to visit my uncle for over a year. He wasn't the easiest person to get along with, especially in his later years. He got angry if you didn't come to visit, but when you did show up, he virtually accused you of being nice to him in hopes of inheriting the house." Michael smiled grimly. "As if anyone would really want it."

"Your sister must, she's moving in here."

"Ah, well that's another story."

When Michael didn't go on, Heather decided that he felt he'd revealed enough family history to a virtual stranger for one morning. Not wanting to put him on the spot with more questions, she poured some primer in her roller tray and turned to go up the ladder.

"Time to get back to work," she announced.

He reached out and put a gentle hand on her arm to prevent her from rushing up the ladder.

"I know this is a bit sudden, but would you be willing to have dinner with me tonight?"

The "no" was already half-formed on her lips when she looked at him. There was such an appealing sweetness about his almost shy smile that she paused. He was the man in the car again, and she felt like they had known each other forever. Don't go out with artists or anyone involved in art even if they do seem nice, she warned herself. It will only end badly.

He smiled at her again.

"I'd be happy to," Heather heard herself say.

Stunned at her own impulsiveness, Heather struggled to pay attention while they agreed to meet at a restaurant that was halfway between the Compton house and her apartment back in Northampton. At least he's not picking me up at my door, she thought, trying to convince herself that this was more of a business dinner than a date.

"I know this is going to sound strange . . ." he began, catching her attention.

Uh, oh, Heather thought, here's where it starts. He's going to want me to dress up all in leather or in a cheer-leader's outfit. Or else he's going to claim that he has no money so can I get the bill this time. Her mind was talking so loudly that she almost missed his words.

"If you should notice anything odd happen around here," Michael said, "I'd appreciate it if you'd let me know."

"Odd in what way?" she managed to ask.

"I can't say exactly." He gave a short laugh. "I don't mean to sound mysterious. Forget I said anything. See you tonight."

With a smile and a quick wave he turned and left the room. No sooner had he left than Abby appeared in the doorway.

"You're early," Heather said.

"Yeah, I got halfway through the job at the restaurant and needed to find out what color they wanted the rest room walls," Abby replied. "The manager was away somewhere, so we have to wait until tomorrow to finish up. Who was that guy who passed me in the hall?"

"Michael Compton."

"The rabid dog's brother?"

Heather nodded.

"Wow! Well, he can clean my paint brushes any time."

Abby glanced over to see if Heather smiled at her comment, but her friend seemed a million miles away.

Shrugging, Abby asked, "So what do you want me to do?"

"There's another can of primer on the other side of the room by the gear. Why don't you start priming one of those peach walls?"

"Sure thing."

Heather went up the ladder and started to roll on the paint.

"Where did you say that other can of paint was?" Abby called from across the room.

"Right in front of you," Heather said.

"Are you sure you brought it in from the truck?"

Groaning to herself at Abby's ability to miss what was right in front of her face, Heather came down the ladder and walked over to her friend.

"It's right . . ." Heather began. But there was no can of paint to be seen. Brushes and an extra ladder, tarps and scrapers, but no second can of paint.

"You see, this time it wasn't my fault," Abby said triumphantly. She started to grin, but stopped when she saw Heather's worried expression. "It's not a big deal, I'm sure I've got a can of primer in my truck. I'll go get it."

Is that the kind of odd happening that Michael was talking about? Heather wondered as she watched Abby leave. She had been positive there had been two cans of primer, but she'd been positive of things before and turned out to be mistaken. She wasn't going to mention this to Michael. Heather didn't want him thinking she was the kind of faint-hearted woman who jumped at every shadow and thought a curtain blowing in the breeze was a ghost. And she certainly wouldn't tell Abby, who would make fun of her, and say that Michael's warning showed that he and Heather were two nuts from the same bowl.

But if things got odder? What then? Well, she'd cross that bridge when she came to it.

## Chapter Three

"It must be time for lunch," Abby said, surveying the wall she had just finished covering with primer.

"Two down and two to go," said Heather. "We're making progress."

"But it's the two long ones that are left. They'll easily take us all afternoon. We need a good lunch to strengthen the inner woman. Let's go to that place we passed up the road. It looked like it would have a good sandwich. Maybe we can split a grinder."

"I should probably stick to a salad," said Heather, thinking about her upcoming dinner.

"Hah! You burn food like a furnace. I'm the one who should be living on bread and water," said Abby, patting her hips.

"Men like women who are filled out in the right places."

28

"Yeah, but it's hard to keep the amount of filling under control."

Heather smiled. "Well, I'll go tell someone we're taking a lunch break."

"Okay, I'll do some cleaning up here and meet you by the front door."

"I wonder how I get to the kitchen. I'll probably find someone there at this hour."

Abby pointed to a door in the corner of the dining room. "That probably leads to the kitchen. This is a dining room, after all, and the servants didn't parade down the main hall with the food."

"Good point."

Heather opened the door and found herself confronted by a hallway. As she walked down the hall she passed a butler's pantry and a couple of rooms that seemed to be used primarily for storage. Where the hall intersected another coming from the front of the house, there was a door to the left. Hearing laughter coming from the room beyond, she tentatively pushed the door open.

Jack and a thin middle-aged woman wearing an apron, whom Heather assumed must be Mrs. Maxwell, the cook, were sitting by a large table in what was obviously the kitchen.

The woman jumped up as Heather entered and looked at her nervously, as if she might be accused of doing something wrong by sitting down in the kitchen. Maybe Caroline Webster had that effect on her staff, thought Heather.

"Hello," Jack said, giving her a lazy smile. "How's the painting coming? Mrs. Maxwell and I were just saying that we'll hardly know the old dining room once it gets a new coat of paint."

Heather smiled. She crossed the room, introduced herself to the cook, and said that she and her partner would be leaving for an hour or so for lunch.

"You're welcome to eat here," Mrs. Maxwell said. "I'm sure we can find some salads and sandwich fixings."

"No thanks. We need to get out in the fresh air after smelling paint all morning."

The woman nodded solemnly as if everything said to her was to be taken with the utmost seriousness.

"Maybe later on this afternoon we could have a pitcher of ice water," said Heather. "It gets warm up by the ceiling and the chemicals can make your throat dry."

"I'll bring you some lemonade," the woman said with a smile, as if pleased to have found a way to be of service.

"That would be great," said Heather.

"Anything else that you need carried?" asked Jack.

"Not today." She paused for a moment before making a decision. "By the way, Jack, did you happen to notice whether we carried one or two cans of paint into the dining room this morning?"

Jack looked across the room for a moment, then shook his head. "I'm not sure. Why? Is there something missing?"

Heather smiled. "Probably just a few of my brain cells."

"Yeah, I know what you mean. Lloyd's always saying that if he wants a tool, all he has to do is look where I was working yesterday because I always forget to return things to the gardener's shed."

"That's probably what happened here too," she said, waving good-bye and leaving the kitchen. She went straight this time, heading back down the hall to the front of the house. She paused in the foyer to look once again at the ornate moldings that ran along the top of the oak wainscotting. A loud voice that she recognized as Caroline's came through a slightly open door to her right.

"Don't you know better, Michael, than to get involved with the hired help? Good lord, she's a painter, who are you going to date next, an automobile mechanic?"

"Don't be such a snob, Caroline," Heather heard Michael say in an amused tone. "She seems like an interesting woman. Anyway, you can't expect me to stay out here with you and have no social life at all."

"And why *did* you decide to join me?" asked Caroline in a suddenly sly tone. "When I first suggested that we do this together, you as much as told me that it was a crazy idea and I was on my own. You said you had no interest in Uncle Leo's house. There was nothing I could say or do to pull you away from Boston and that precious little fiancée of yours. What happened? Has that little love boat gone on the rocks?"

"Stay out of my personal life, Caroline," Michael said softly, but with a hint of warning. "It has nothing to do with you."

Footsteps headed for the closed door, so Heather quickly made her way out the front.

"Ready to chow down?" asked Abby, who was leaning against one of the large cement flower pots next to the driveway.

"Let's get out of here," Heather said shortly, almost running towards the van. Abby hurried to catch up.

They sat in the back of the roadside sandwich place eating at a wooden picnic table. Heather told Abby about her date with Michael and the conversation she had overheard between Michael and Caroline.

"I knew I shouldn't get involved with anyone who has anything to do with art," Heather concluded. She threw a piece of bread from her sandwich to a nearby squirrel, who ducked as the bread flew past him like a fastball.

"That makes sense," said Abby. "You should only date guys that you've got nothing in common with, except maybe for a physical attraction. My mom always told me that was the foundation of a good long-term relationship. Skip the conversation and get right to the good stuff."

Heather grinned in spite of herself.

"Do you know anything about plumbing?" Abby asked.

Heather shook her head.

"That's perfect, then. Find a cute plumber and you'll be all set. I hear they make a pretty good living too."

"Okay, okay, I get your point," Heather said. "Since all I know about is art, I'm naturally going to be attracted to men with the same interest."

"Bingo!"

Heather sighed. "It's just that ever since Richard and I broke up . . ."

Abby waved the hand that held her grinder. "I know, I know. He was a painter, and once his paintings started to sell he ran off to New York and never came back. But that was Richard. The guy was a bum. He was living off of you and at the same time made fun of your business. Maybe Michael will be different."

"It's just that I wasted almost two years with Richard, encouraging him, getting his work in shows, writing his publicity."

"And he hardly stayed around to say thanks," said Abby. "I know that stinks, but what did you want from the guy: gratitude or love? He didn't love you, so it's just as well he wasn't more polite or you'd still be doing his laundry. In my opinion he couldn't love anyone but himself. You're better off without him."

"So why should Michael be different?"

"For one thing, he's got a job, and he's already made something of himself. He won't be trying to use you as a way to get ahead. And, who knows, maybe he's more mature."

Heather smiled. "Are you saying I should be looking for an unattached senior citizen?"

"Did I ever tell you about my Aunt Sadie who married the guy thirty years older than herself?"

Heather raised her hand. "I've heard the story. But what about Michael having a fiancée? That doesn't sound very encouraging."

"Maybe they split up. The only way you'll find out is by going out with him tonight and asking."

"I can't admit that I was eavesdropping on his conversation with his sister," said Heather.

Abby gave her a don't-be-so-dim look. "Work the conversation around to it. Two people out on a first date: it's natural to ask if he's ever been married, engaged, had his tonsils out, or whatever you want to ask."

Heather frowned. "I guess I just don't like invading people's privacy. I don't like answering personal questions, so I don't like to ask them."

"Just ask him questions. If he asks you any that make you uncomfortable, give an evasive answer. It always works for me. I've even pretended not to remember my age when a guy asks."

"You've given so many different answers to that question, you probably don't know what the right one is anymore," said Heather with a grin.

"So what, age is a state of mind," Abby said, throwing

her soda cup in the garbage and standing up to leave. "Look, go out with this guy, find out whatever you can, then make up your mind. His package looks nice, now you've got to explore the inner man."

Heather shook her head. "That sounds tricky."

"Nah! That's the part that's fun."


"Hold it!" Abby shouted as Heather started to turn the van through the gate that led to the Compton House.

"What's the matter?"

"Look at that," Abby said, pointing.

To the left of the gate, the sturdy wooden post that held the mailbox was leaning to one side. The black metal box itself had come loose from the post and lay on the grass by the side of the road. Abby jumped out of the car and picked it up. She stopped for a moment, examining the post.

"Tire tread marks," she said as she got back in the van carrying the dented box. "Somebody hit that post with a vehicle of some sort."

"Maybe it happened at night. It could have been dark and somebody missed the turn."

Abby shook her head. "It was fine when I came over here this morning. And I think I'd have noticed it when we left for lunch."

"You mean it happened in the last hour?" said Heather.

"Yeah. And I don't think it was somebody with a vision problem. I think it was done on purpose."

"Probably some kid's prank. It happens all the time out in the country," said Heather.

Abby looked doubtful. "In the middle of the day?"

Heather didn't answer. She was too busy wondering

if this was the type of odd happening that Michael had in mind.

Since the front door was open, Abby and Heather didn't bother to ring the bell, figuring there was no sense in disturbing the maid just to let them in after lunch. They went down the hall to the dining room and Abby put the mailbox on the floor with their painting equipment.

"I guess we should notify somebody that they won't be getting any mail today," said Abby.

"I'll go. I've pretty much figured out the route to the kitchen," said Heather, heading for the doorway.

Before she could reach it, Caroline Webster entered the room with her husband slowly following a few steps behind.

"This is wretched! Wretched! I thought you were going to paint the room blue. That was bad enough, but this ghastly white just won't do."

Heather heard Abby giggle behind her.

"That's only the primer coat, Mrs. Webster," Heather said gently. "We wanted to make sure that the blue would go on evenly and have something to adhere to."

"That's what I told you, Caroline," Mr. Webster said.

Caroline sniffed. "Well, I'm still not convinced that blue is the best color for this room."

"It will be fine," her husband assured her.

She walked into the middle of the room and wrapped her arms around her thin body. She stared up at the walls with apprehension as if afraid that they were going to close in and attack her.

"There is one problem," Abby said.

Caroline Webster turned to her husband with an I-told-you-so look.

Abby picked the mailbox off of the floor and held it up.

"Someone knocked down your mailbox," she announced.

"Oh, George!" Caroline wailed, scurrying across the room to stand next to her husband.

"There's nothing to worry about," he said with a patient smile. "Probably just a couple of local lads having some fun. In Boston they would steal your car, here they only damage your mailbox."

Abby opened her mouth to express her opinion that it was more than that, but a sharp glance from Heather silenced her.

"I'm sure you're right," said Heather.

A nervous smile played across Caroline's face. "Do you really think that's all it is, George?"

"Of course." He walked over and took the mailbox from Abby. "I'll just give this to Lloyd and tell him to put it back up." He put his arm around his wife. "See you later, ladies," he said to Abby and Heather as he gently led his wife out into the hall.

"Wow!" Abby whispered. "I've never seen anyone that upset about a mailbox."

Heather frowned. "Well, she is kind of a nervous person."

"Nervous doesn't begin to describe her," said Abby as she opened a can of primer and poured some in her bucket. "But at least it took her mind off our paint job."

Heather nodded and began pouring some paint in her bucket as well. They placed their ladders on opposite sides of the room and began to paint. Watching the dirty dark peach color disappear beneath a fresh coat of white primer soon began to soothe Heather's mind. One of the things she liked about painting was the immediate gratification from seeing a room almost instantly transformed. The dark, forbidding dining room of this morning had already been changed into a brighter, more cheerful space.

When she paused for a moment after working steadily for over an hour, and glanced behind her at the length of the room, she felt that this was a place that could be both elegant and comfortable with the right paint, furniture, and decorations. Maybe—just maybe—she thought, staring upward, it would be possible to convince Caroline Webster to let her paint a mural on the ceiling. Something that would bring the view from outside into the dining room and at the same time make the rather large room feel more cozy. But it will take a lot of convincing, Heather thought.

Jack and Mrs. Maxwell came in. A bright smile lit up Jack's face as soon as he saw that Heather had spotted him. Jack was carrying a small table, and the cook had a tray with a pitcher and glasses.

"Time for a break, you guys," Jack announced.

Heather and Abby came down from their ladders, and Heather introduced Abby to the gardener and the cook. Mrs. Maxwell quickly excused herself with some mumbled comment about checking on something cooking in the kitchen. Jack, however, poured a glass of lemonade for each of the women and one for himself. He finished his in a couple of gulps.

"Is it hot working out in the garden?" asked Heather.

"Nah, the garden wouldn't be so bad, but old Lloyd made me pull out that mailbox post. That works up a sweat. Then he got me to dig a new hole closer to the gate where it won't be so easy to hit," said Jack. "I told him that it won't make any difference. If somebody wants to take out that mailbox, they're gonna do it no matter how careful we are."

"Do you think someone hit it on purpose?" asked Heather.

"Sure. That post has been there for probably thirty years and no one had any trouble avoiding it before. It was set so far back that you'd have to go out of your way to knock it down."

"Why would anyone want to do that?" asked Abby.

Jack looked off toward the back windows as if trying to decide how much to say.

"Well, Leo Compton wasn't exactly the most popular guy in town."

"What did he do?" asked Heather.

"It was more what he didn't do, from what I've heard. He never gave to charity or did anything for the town. And he tried to get the town council to reject that condominium complex they built on the other side of the hill a couple of years ago. Leo said he didn't want a bunch of folks from the city having summer places up here and ruining the neighborhood."

"What happened?"

"The town council decided that they needed the taxes, I guess, so it got built."

"But why knock over the mailbox now? After all, Leo Compton is dead," asked Heather.

"I heard that the same guy who developed those condos wanted to buy this property for a golf course. I think folks in town were pretty sure that was going to happen until Mrs. Webster decided to fix up the place. A golf course would bring new business into the area, so I guess the locals aren't too keen on Caroline Webster either."

"But would they care enough to vandalize a mailbox?" asked Abby. "That seems kind of extreme."

"Yeah," Jack agreed. "But from what I've heard in town, when the Comptons owned the mill, they weren't exactly the best people to work for."

"But they haven't had that mill for over thirty years," said Heather, recalling her library research.

Jack smiled. "I guess people have long memories out here. Heck, there isn't that much to do but to sit around and remember. Most of the kids leave town as soon as they graduate from high school, and the ones that stay around keep hearing the same old stories. I guess it isn't surprising that once in a while they get bored and decide to go after the Comptons."

"Makes me kind of glad that I grew up in a city," said Abby.

"Yeah, well I gotta get back to work or Lloyd will come looking for me."

"What do you think?" Heather asked when Jack had left the room.

"He's cute but way too young," said Abby.

Heather gave Abby a poke in the arm. "No, I meant his story about the mailbox. Do you buy it?"

"Maybe. But it sounds kind of paranoid to me. I still like the teenage prank theory. What about you?"

"I don't know. But if anything else happens, then I might agree that Jack has a point."

"Yeah, well let's hope nothing else happens until we're out of here."

The rest of the afternoon passed quietly. By five o'clock, Heather and Abby were standing back to back in the center of the room admiring their completed job.

"Let it dry overnight, and tomorrow we can apply the blue," said Heather.

"Remember, I won't be here in the morning. I've still got to finish the rest rooms in that restaurant. If the manager shows up early enough, I'll be back here right after lunch." Abby studied the walls. "We still might need to use two coats of blue. These old plaster walls absorb a lot of paint."

Heather nodded. "Well, I'll just keep working away at it until you get here."

"Maybe Michael will come by tomorrow to keep you company."

"Who knows. After tonight's date he may not be interested anymore."

"That's certainly the wrong attitude," Abby said, starting to clean up her equipment.

Not saying anything, Heather squatted down beside her. They quickly finished sealing the paint cans and rinsed the brushes and rollers in a bucket they'd filled with water at an outside spigot. Then together they rolled up their canvas tarp.

"Guess we can leave this stuff right here," said Abby.

"We'll leave the ladders, but let's put the small stuff in the van."

Abby gave her a quizzical glance.

"The door is never locked and there are so many people wandering around in this house, I think we should be security conscious."

"Okay," Abby said with a shrug. "Although, anybody who would steal a can of paint must be pretty desperate."

Heather bit her lip, but didn't say anything. No point in having Abby think she was as paranoid as Jack with his band of vengeful mailbox pillagers.

They got most of their gear in the van in a couple of trips. Two rollers and a tray remained, and Abby offered to go back by herself to pick them up while Heather organized the stuff in the back of the van. Climbing out of the van, Heather looked at the bay windows in the front of the dining room to make sure they had left them open so the room would air out.

Heather blinked. A shadowy figure standing by the windows was staring out at her. She blinked again and the figure disappeared.

"All set," Abby said, coming out the front door.

"Yes . . . was there anyone in the dining room?"

"Just now?"

"Yeah, right now while you were in there?" Heather asked, hearing a hint of anxiety in her tone.

Abby gave her an odd look. "I didn't see anyone. Why? Did you notice something?"

Heather ran a hand over her eyes. "No. I guess not. It must have been a shadow by the front window."

"Must have been," Abby said, walking around and opening the door to the passenger's side of the van. "One thing this place has got is shadows to spare. Spend a whole day working here and you start to suspect there are monsters in every corner."

Heather climbed into the van beside Abby. As they pulled around the driveway and away from the house, Heather turned to glance back.

"Don't worry about it," said Abby. "Your date tonight will chase away all the shadows."

Heather smiled and wondered if that was true.

## Chapter Four

Heather stood in the pine paneled lobby of the Berkshire Inn, watching the fire crackle and hiss in the large fieldstone fireplace. She had arrived early at the restaurant they had agreed upon because she was uncertain how long it would take her to navigate the twisting roads through the hills from Northampton. But the trip had proven both scenic and easy, so now Heather waited awkwardly, aware that to some men arriving early might make her appear overanxious.

"Never show up on time, in fact always show up late," Abby once advised. "If you arrive even ten minutes late, the guy waiting will always assume it's because one of your many other boyfriends called you at the last minute and begged you to run off for a weekend in Paris with him."

"And is it good if he thinks that?" Heather had asked.

"Of course," Abby replied. "A guy will always try harder if he knows there's competition."

Heather sighed to herself. That sort of game might work fine for Abby, but she became tired at the very thought of it. You had to play enough games in your business life without having it be part of your personal life as well. She had worn her best dark-green linen slacks with a chocolate-brown silk blouse that helped to set off her light complexion, and that was as much of the game as she was willing to play.

"Fires can be hypnotic."

Heather turned and saw Michael standing a few feet away watching her. No longer wearing his mover's clothes, he had on slacks that were earth brown in color and a loden-green shirt that deepened the rich brown of his eyes. He was wearing a coat made of soft leather.

"Were you standing there watching me?" she asked.

He smiled. "You reminded me of something."

"Not Diana again."

"No. I think it was a Rossetti painting. You had an ethereal look about you, staring into the fire like that."

"I see. Well, since I'm tall and thin with rather long features like most of Rossetti's women, I'd say you are starting to see me with a more realistic eye."

"I didn't mean to imply anything negative," Michael said with a worried expression. "That was supposed to be a compliment."

Heather studied him in the flickering firelight. It wasn't his rich wavy hair, chiseled features, or lively brown eyes that caught her attention the most. It was rather the embarrassed smile that played over his mouth as he looked down at her that made her heart jump. He clearly cared about what she thought of him. There wasn't any of the take-it-or-leave-it arrogance typical of so many handsome men. She stuck out her hand.

"We're doing it again, aren't we?" she said.

He gave her a puzzled look but took her hand in his own. The warmth of his touch quickly traveled up her arm.

"We're starting off on the wrong foot again," she explained a bit breathlessly.

He smiled and reluctantly released her hand.

"I promise not to compare you to any work of art for the rest of the evening if you'll allow me to use any other type of compliment I might desire."

"Agreed," Heather said, surprised to realize that she was grinning madly. "And I think my ethereal look is probably due to hunger, so why don't we go into the dining room."

The hostess seated them by a large window. It looked out on the narrow lawn behind the inn that quickly disappeared into a forest of pine trees. The sun setting behind the tall, straight pines outlined the clouds with a pinkish glow.

"That's something you don't get to see in Boston," Michael commented.

"But there are lots of things in Boston that you don't find out here," said Heather, remembering Abby's admonition to take her opportunity to probe.

"True. However I've seen most of those things, but I haven't experienced this. At least not in a long while."

"Have you been in Boston long?"

"Eight years. I did my graduate work there, and then got a job at the museum right out of school." Michael paused and turned to look out the window again, suddenly sad. "It seemed like a dream come true."

"But it wasn't?"

"At first I enjoyed it a great deal. There was so much to learn and I was finally applying some of the things I had studied in school. But gradually I realized that there was a lot of politics in the Boston museum scene, and to get ahead after a certain point, you had to present yourself in the right way to the right people." He smiled. "I know, I know, that's true of any job. But Boston can still be very stuffy at times. I guess I sort of burned out."

"So you took a leave of absence," said Heather. "Do you think you'll go back?" And maybe take up with your fiancée again, she wanted to ask but didn't.

"Depends on what I find out here," he said, giving her a long look.

Heather felt herself redden. "Well, you won't find a museum on every corner, but I'm sure there are other opportunities."

The waitress came to their table to take their order, and Heather wondered whether she had read too much into Michael's expression.

"Partly, of course, I'm also here to help Caroline settle into the Compton House," he continued after the waitress left.

"George Webster told Abby and me that had something to do with Leo Compton's will."

"That's right. Old Uncle Leo was quite a character. About five years ago, he had his attorney send a letter to all of his relatives saying that the house and the surrounding fifty acres would go to any of his remaining blood relatives who were willing to take up residence in the house within a month after the final probate of his will, and who remained in continual residence there for at least three months. If no one met those terms, the executor was directed to sell the estate and disperse the money to a number of charities."

"How many relatives are there?"

"Well, there were three brothers: Leo, Anthony, and Alex. Uncle Leo had no children. Since my father and mother died nine years ago, there are only Caroline and myself left from our branch. Alex moved to Alaska almost twenty years ago. He married out there, someone named Denise, I think, but I've never met her. They had a son, Andrew. But Alex and Andrew died in a boating accident three years ago."

"So you and Caroline are the only remaining relatives?"

"As far as we know." Michael gave an exaggerated shrug as if none of it mattered.

"But isn't the place valuable?" Heather asked in surprise.

"You've seen the house. It's a real money pit. Who could afford to renovate it except someone like George Webster."

"Didn't Uncle Leo leave any money in his will so someone could fix the place up?"

Michael shook his head. "When my grandfather, Reginald Compton, died, he left the house to his oldest son, Leo. The money, which didn't amount to a fortune, was divided up equally among the three brothers. My dad put his into the lumber business he had. When he sold out after he got sick, most of it went into nursing home care for my mother. Uncle Alex, or so the story goes, lost most of his in some Alaskan oil scheme. Uncle Leo lived off of his."

"He never worked?" Heather asked.

"Uncle Leo trained to be a lawyer, because his father insisted that he have a profession, but he never went into practice. I guess what he inherited along with the house was enough, given the frugal way he lived."

"But what about the land? Isn't it valuable? I heard something about an offer being made to buy the property for a golf course."

Michael laughed. "Ah, you've heard that one already too. That offer disappeared from the table a long time ago. But according to Uncle Leo, developers were always coming around and offering him a fortune for the property. That might be true, but I really don't want to get involved. Anyway, Caroline plans to live there and keep the property together."

"Even if the money doesn't matter to you, don't you want a share of the house? It could be a wonderful place."

"Hmm. I guess there's just more family history there than I feel really comfortable with. The Comptons weren't always nice people. When the mill was still going, there were constant problems between the Comptons and the townspeople who worked there. And it didn't get much better after that. My grandfather took what he could from the town and didn't give much back. Uncle Leo carried on the same tradition. I don't want to live in a place where people hate me for my family name."

"Well, I can certainly understand that," Heather said.

"I'm only staying to help Caroline for the required three months. After that Caroline and George can buy me out for a nominal amount, and my sister will become the sole owner. Caroline sees herself as some kind of local aristocrat. Now that she's got George's money to back her up, she wants to fix the place up and live out here at least part of the year."

Their food came and they ate in silence for a while.

"What about you?" Michael asked. "If I dare to bring the subject up again, why is someone with a fine arts degree painting houses?"

"Have you ever heard of Clarissa Martinson?"

"The portrait painter. Of course I have, I think we have one of her works in the museum." He snapped his fingers. "Is she a relative?"

"My mother," Heather said.

"Ah, so you don't want to walk in your mother's footsteps. I guess after what I've just said about wanting to desert the family home, I can't really criticize you."

"It's not just that," Heather responded. "I really like doing decorative painting. Lots of people would say it's not art, but they haven't seen some of the designs I've created and painted for my customers' homes. They're every bit as artistic as daubing paint on a canvas. And when you cover a wall or ceiling, you change the entire atmosphere of a room more than you'll ever do with a three-by-five painting."

"How much of your work is like that and how much is . . ."

"Just slapping paint on walls?" said Heather, her eyes flashing a bit.

"I wasn't going to put it exactly that way, but yes. How much of it is less artistic?"

Heather paused. "Most of it is pretty run-of-the-mill: covering a wall with paint or copying a stencil pattern. But I'm convinced that the longer we stay in business and develop a reputation, the more we'll get jobs that require using our artistic skills. And you know a lot of 'real' artists, even famous people like my mother, spend most of their time doing pictures just meant to please the person who's paying."

"I know," Michael said, nodding. "The history of art certainly shows that unless he or she is born rich, an artist has to paint for an audience. I think you've found a great way to make a living and at the same time be creative."

He reached out and gave her hand a squeeze. Surprised, Heather found herself responding.

"What does your mother think?" he asked.

"She's coming around to it. At first she thought I was squandering my talent, as she put it. I had won a couple of contests in college, and Mom was convinced that I had inherited her ability. She wanted me to rent a studio, do more advanced study, and try to break into the art scene. Mom figured that some of her contacts would help. But I knew that just wasn't me. I've always been fascinated by houses, and this is what I want to do."

"Does your father share your mother's views?"

Heather laughed. "He teaches chemistry, so he stays out of the discussion. All he says to my Mom is, 'Let the girl do what she wants, Clari.'"

"I don't think anyone gets the girl to do anything else," Michael said with a small smile.

Heather grinned. "I'm not stubborn, just determined. I want to succeed at this."

"I guess you get some support from your partner."

"Abby's great. We met in college when we had the same class on drawing the male nude. I was lucky to pass, she kept me laughing so much. But she's really very artistic and lots of fun to work with."

"And I imagine the job at the Compton House might help you," said Michael.

"If your sister likes my work and tells other people about it."

"I'll see that she does."

Heather paused, unsure how far to take the offer of help. "And I was kind of hoping that maybe she'd let me be a little more creative. I'd really like to do some art work on the ceiling in the dining room."

"And I can think of a wall in the front parlor that would benefit by having a distinctive mural," said Michael. "Leave Caroline to me. She owes me a favor, and she's not as difficult as she seems. It's just that some things have been happening recently that have gotten her upset."

"Like the smashed mailbox?" Heather suggested.

"That's right, you and Abby were the ones who found that." Michael said and paused as if reluctant to say more.

"You mentioned something this morning about being on the lookout for odd occurrences. Why did you say that?"

Michael studied the plate in front of him for a moment as if trying to reach a decision.

"Look, you have to keep this to yourself because Caroline and George are the only ones who know about it, and they want it kept a secret. Although I wouldn't be surprised if the whole town knew by now."

Heather nodded.

"Well, it started about a month ago when Caroline announced her decision to move into the Compton House. She has been receiving threats."

"What kind of threats?"

"At first they were letters sent to her home in Boston. Words cut out of magazines telling her that the town didn't want any more Comptons living there, and not to move into the Compton House if she valued her life."

"What did she do? Did she go to the police?"

"There are no real police in Compton anymore since the population shrank thirty years ago after the mill closed. There are two part-timers who handle traffic violations, but the state police take care of any criminal investigations. George took it to them, and they said to let them know if anything more serious happened. They figured it was just a nasty prank."

"I guess it could be," admitted Heather.

"But then . . . but then a week ago, it was the first night she spent in the house, right after the will was probated. She went out to supper with George and when they came back someone had written 'Get Out' on the wall in their bedroom in what looked like blood."

"Blood! What did the state police say to that?"

"They came in and looked for fingerprints and took a sample of the blood for analysis. There were no prints belonging to anyone outside of the house, and the blood turned out to be from a pig. They said they would ask some questions in the neighborhood, but the state police don't know the town of Compton any more than we do. Those that have stayed in the town keep pretty much to themselves."

Heather looked out the window. Where there had been a serene sunset, there was now complete darkness. Only by looking against the slightly lighter sky could she make out the sharp tops of the pine trees.

"Is that why you came out here? To look after your sister? To keep her safe?"

Michael smiled. "Partly, although you make me sound more heroic than I am. I also wanted to get out of Boston for the reasons that I've already told you and for a few others."

Like a fiancée, Heather thought.

"And since George's business keeps him in Boston much of the time, I just thought I'd try to help her over the rough spots. I imagine that once the locals see that she's determined to stay, they'll give up."

Heather nodded, not at all sure that Michael wasn't being too optimistic.

An hour later, after they had turned down the offerings of the dessert cart and had a leisurely cup of coffee, they walked out into the parking lot.

"Well, I guess I'll see you tomorrow," Heather said.

"Let me at least walk you to your chariot," said Michael, heading in the direction of her van.

Heather was about to say that wouldn't be necessary when a cold blast of wind whistled eerily through the pines and made an escort seem like a good idea.

"What do you call your company?" asked Michael.

"Passionate Painters," mumbled Heather, wishing as she often did, that she had not allowed Abby to choose the company name.

"Do I dare to ask whether you're passionate about things other than painting?"

Heather turned toward him, a tart response already forming on her tongue, when the heel of her shoe twisted on the rough gravel of the parking lot, throwing her off-balance. Immediately a strong arm was around her to keep her from falling. She tried to right herself without his help, and overcompensated. Suddenly she found herself pressing her body into his. As she looked up to get her bearings, his lips were suddenly there and somehow hers were pressing gently into them. Heather couldn't remember making a decision about all this, but somehow, for a moment, that didn't seem to matter.

When his head moved back, she was thankful it was dark and he couldn't see the confusion on her face.

"Sorry, I'm sure I've just done something wrong again," he said.

Heather hobbled across the parking lot to her van.

"Thanks for dinner," she said, hopping up into the seat.

"My pleasure. But you could at least tell me you aren't angry," he said. She thought she detected amusement in his tone.

"I'll let you know tomorrow," she replied. "After I've had a chance to think about it."

## Chapter Five

"Let me get this straight," Abby said the next morning as they were loading the vans. "You kissed him and then got angry because he kissed you back. I'll have to try that. I'll kiss some cute guy, then slap his face and say, 'Don't you try getting fresh with me, buster!' "

"It didn't happen exactly like that," said Heather, suppressing a smile. "It was more of a mutual kiss."

"Ah, an important difference. But I still don't see why you're so angry: a nice guy takes you to dinner, walks you to your car, and keeps you from falling. Why begrudge him a little kiss?"

"It's not the kiss that bothers me."

"What? You didn't like the dinner?" asked Abby, throwing a tarp into the van.

Heather stopped working and faced her friend. "I'm not sure why it is. Maybe it's because I'm here painting walls for a living and I don't need some handsome rich guy who spends all his time floating around a museum rescuing me from a life of turpentine and ladders."

Abby took a step back. "Whoa! Do we have a little class warfare here? And don't you think you're jumping to conclusions? Just because the Comptons were once the robber barons of the eastern Berkshires doesn't mean that Michael is rich. Sister Caroline seems to be getting by on her husband's money, but as far as we know, Michael has been working for a living. Right?"

"Yes."

"And there's no reason to assume that Michael is trying to rescue you from anything. You said that he complimented you on our business. Just because the late, unlamented Richard thought you were slumming it by painting walls in order to support him while he dabbled in derivative Cubism, that's no reason to believe that Michael shares Richard's bad attitude. Give the guy a chance. Don't condemn him without a trial."

Heather frowned and stared hard at the pyramid of paint cans she had arranged by the rear of her van.

"Okay. You're right," she finally said. "Maybe I'm letting my leftover anger toward Richard ruin my chances with Michael. Of course, there's still the little matter of Michael's fiancée."

Abby shut the back doors of her van. She walked around and climbed into the driver's seat.

"Yeah, you still need to work on your interrogation techniques. But you'll be seeing him today. I'm sure that dynamite kiss you gave him last night has softened him up, so he'll answer any question you ask. Hit him with it today while his knees are still weak."

Heather grinned. "I just might try that."

"Wish me luck with those restaurant johns," Abby said, and with a wave out the window she pulled away from the small warehouse space that she and Heather rented for their gear.

Heather loaded five gallons of the blue dining room paint into the back of the van, and in a few minutes she was heading over the hills toward Compton.

It's amazing how much better I feel after talking to Abby, Heather thought as she drove. I guess she's right, I'm still carrying an awful lot of baggage around with me from my time with Richard. And why not just ask Michael if he's seriously involved with someone? After all, if you take a woman to dinner and give her a fairly romantic kiss, that would be a natural question for her to ask. Heather smiled to herself at the thought of getting her relationship with Michael on some kind of firm footing, and tried, not for the first time, to remember exactly how that kiss had happened and what precisely it had felt like.

Abby would tell me that if my memory is fading, I should just do it again, Heather thought, and found herself laughing out loud in the rattling van.

When she pulled up in front of the Compton House, her good mood faded. She had put the threats against Caroline out of her mind, and hadn't felt that she could tell Abby about them because of her promise to Michael to keep it secret. But seeing the house staring down bleakly at her brought the chill of last night's revelations rushing back like the sun sliding under a cloud, and she was relieved to see Michael come through the doorway as she opened the van doors.

"I see that even a curator on leave sees fit to get up with the birds," she joked.

His face clouded and she was afraid she had offended him.

"I'm sorry . . ." she began, not sure what she was apologizing for.

He took her arm and drew her around to the side of the van away from the house. He stepped close, so close she could smell his after-shave and see the small spot on his chin that he had missed while shaving. She wanted to reach up and touch it, but decided that might be going too far.

"Something happened," he whispered.

"Another threat?"

"Worse. The maid, Anna, went out last night. I think she has a boyfriend who lives a few miles away. She parked her car around the back and was walking up the path to let herself in through the kitchen door when someone jumped her."

"What happened?" asked Heather. "Is she all right?"

Michael nodded. "Whoever it was gave her a hard push. Anna fell and then her assailant ran off. She was only shaken up. But she quit. She's upstairs packing now. I guess Caroline had told her about the earlier threats, so this was enough to really scare her."

"Is her quitting a big problem?" asked Heather. She couldn't imagine that the rather uppity maid had ever done very much anyway.

"She was something of a companion for Caroline. We have a professional service coming in from Pittsfield twice a week to clean, but Caroline needs some female companionship. She may seem quite strong, but underneath it all, she's rather fragile."

"There is Mrs. Maxwell."

"Yes," Michael said with a small smile, "but that poor woman is so nervous that if Caroline just glances in her direction she cringes. I've been on the phone with

George trying to arrange for a new maid, but apparently these things take time. Checking references and all."

Heather looked at Michael's worried face. Only a good, decent man would be so concerned about his sister. What if she offered to stay at the house for a few days? Heather thought. She would be there all day painting anyway, it would be just as easy to spend the night and get an early start on the job in the morning. It also meant that there would be the chance to spend time with Michael in a more normal setting than the average date. On the other hand, the idea of being a nursemaid to Caroline wasn't appealing. Heather had to admit, however, that she felt a little sorry for the nervous, uptight woman. And if she and Michael did develop into something, Caroline would be her sister-in-law and . . . Heather quickly reined in her wild imaginings.

She presented her plan to Michael.

"It's very kind of you to offer," he said, frowning, "but with everything that's been going on here lately, I'm just not sure. I'll be away on business during the day, and Jack and Lloyd are out in the garden most of the time. I'm not sure how much help Mrs. Maxwell would be in an emergency."

"All that's happened so far are minor acts of vandalism. We don't even know if the attack on Anna was related to the threats against Caroline."

"Well, since you are going to be here all day painting," Michael said slowly.

"And I promise that I won't take any chances. The first sign of anything dangerous, Caroline and I are out of here. And you'll be back in the evening."

His eyes met hers with a look that showed he wanted to spend more time with her as well, and that it had only been his concern for her safety that had made him reluctant to accept her offer right away.

"It's a deal, then," he said, and gave her an impulsive hug.

Still savoring the feeling of his body against her own, Heather said, "But I'll have to explain to Abby what's going on. She'll wonder why I've suddenly decided to take up residence here."

Michael sighed. "Tell her the whole story. I think any attempt to maintain secrecy disappeared when Anna was attacked. I wouldn't be surprised if she tried to sue us for negligence. By the end of today it will probably be all over Berkshire County. The best we can hope for is that being two hours from Boston, none of the larger papers will get wind of it."

They walked into the front hallway. Heather looked up at the marvelously carved moldings two floors above her head. Surely that ceiling had been painted white once, she thought. Now it was a yellowed, waxy color that only increased the gloom in the foyer.

"Still think it's a marvelous old house?" asked Michael.

"Oh, yes," said Heather. "After all, it wasn't the house that jumped out at Anna last night."

"I wish we knew who it was."

Heather turned to go down the side hall to the dining room.

"I have to go to the state police barracks to file a report and run a few other errands," said Michael, "but I'll be back some time this afternoon. You'll probably want to knock off early and go home to get some things for the next few nights."

"Okay," Heather said and waved good-bye as Michael went down the back hall toward the kitchen.

Her first impression upon entering the dining room was surprise at how bright it looked in the morning. Even though it was only primer, the white paint had certainly dispelled the gloom that seemed to permeate the rest of the house. She was glad that the blue she had chosen was mixed heavily with white, so the overall impression would be of luminescence. That kind of glow would be exactly right for this room.

She went over and examined her equipment. Everything seemed to be exactly as she and Abby had left it yesterday. Their two twelve-foot wooden stepladders were still stacked against the back wall under the window. Wooden ladders were heavy to carry around, but both she and Abby preferred them for their stability and long life. Heather bent over to lift one and heard the sound of voices from outside come floating through the open window.

"You shouldn't have done it," said a man's voice that was familiar but not entirely recognizable.

"It worked, didn't it?" a muffled, female voice replied. "We have time."

"Not enough," said the woman.

There was silence. After a few seconds Heather risked poking her head up above the window frame. No one was there, but in the distance, behind the grape trellis, she saw someone walking away toward the gardens.

Not daring to try to find her way outside through the kitchen, Heather tore out the front door and ran around the house. When she reached the window where she had heard the conversation, she paused a moment to get her bearings, then walked swiftly over to the trellis. A narrow, overgrown path led through thicket of bushes and off in the direction of what she thought must be the gardens. Hoping to catch sight of the man who had been talking under the window, Heather hurried down the path. When she reached the other side of the bushes, she could see a building in the distance. Guessing that he was heading there, she picked up her pace.

A small circular clearing opened up in front of her and Heather paused for a moment in the center. Three paths went off in different directions. Which one should I take? she wondered.

The suddenness with which the ground gave way beneath her feet took her breath away. If she had been any nearer to the center of the hole, it would have been a straight drop. Instead her chest hit the edge of the opening hard enough to make her gasp, and she slowly slid over the edge.

Her hands and feet began frantically groping for something to stop her descent, but the sky was a circle of light several feet above her head before her feet found a narrow purchase and her fingertips managed to cling to a protruding few inches of stone.

She hung there, her toes pushing tensely against the wall, her fingernails sliding on the smooth wet stone. Where am I, she thought desperately. Not daring to move very much, she took a quick glance over her left shoulder. A long narrow cylinder led down to a reflection in the water below. A well! She had fallen into an old well!

Soon my muscles will cramp and then I'll fall, she thought. How far down is the water? What difference does it make? If the water is deep enough so I won't be killed by the fall, I'll just bob around until I drown anyway! A blind panic came over her and she screamed for help. A shadow seemed to pass over the opening above her. Someone looking down? When she risked an upward glance, there was a fleeting image, then nothing but the beautiful, impassive blue of the sky.

"Help!" she called again. But the face didn't return.

Got to stay calm, she told herself. She looked down again. Her right foot was on a stone block of the well lining that stuck out about three inches; her left foot rested on a bit less. She was only a little over three feet from the top, about a foot beyond the reach of her arms. Could she climb out? In the dim light she couldn't see any footholds that would allow her to escape. Her fingers were clinging to two inches of slippery rock, so there was no way she could simply pull herself up.

She called for help again. This time, she hoped, in a calmer tone. She waited a moment, then called again. How often was this path used? Even if someone heard her . . . she paused, recalling the face that had disappeared. Was there any guarantee that person would even want to rescue her?

A sense of vertigo swept over her. She could feel her body beginning to lean into the center of the hole as if it had given up on the project of survival and was ready to have the ordeal come to an end. She shook her head, refusing to yield, and pushed hard into the wall, digging her nails painfully into small ledge as if by sheer will power she could make her way up the wall. She called out again.

Find a way to rest, she thought. If I go on like this I'll be too tired to hold on. My calf muscles are already starting to cramp. If I lose my footing . . . I have to close my eyes and lean into the wall. Stretch one leg and then the other. She paused and called out for help again.

"Heather?" His voice was so close and the response so unexpected that she almost let go.

"Michael! I need help to get out of here."

"Hang on. I'll be right back with a rope."

"Please hurry."

Stretch one leg, then the other, she repeated to herself. Time passed, and she focused on keeping her legs moving. First one, then the other. "Here comes the rope, Heather, there's a loop in one end. Put it around your body and under your arms."

His voice was calm, almost soft, but there was an urgency in it like the humming of electricity in the wires.

"I'm not sure I can hold on with only one hand."

"I'll reach down and hold your free hand and help slide the rope over. Put the rope over your head then under one arm. Then let go and put it under the other arm."

Heather slowly released her grip on the wall with her left hand. She caught the rope. Michael, who was hanging halfway over the edge of the well, grabbed her hand and helped put the rope under her arm. Then she released her other hand and got the loop around her body.

"Good. Now lean back into the rope. Don't worry. I've got it secured, so you can't fall very far. Use your feet and I'll help pull you up."

What Heather had expected to be a long slow climb, similar to those trudges up Mount Everest that she'd seen on television was over in a matter of seconds. Before she knew it, her right foot was at the top of the well and Michael was pulling her free of the hole.

He pulled her into his arms and pressed her tightly against him. He was holding her so close that she could hardly breathe. She drew away from him slightly but stayed in his arms until she trusted herself to speak.

"Are you okay?" he asked hoarsely, and she could hear the concern in his voice.

She nodded and stepped away from him, stumbling slightly before she got her balance.

"What is that?" Heather finally asked in a shaky voice, looking over her shoulder at the hole in the ground

"The stable well. This was all part of the old stable yard and they used that well to water the horses. It's been covered over for years, but I guess the wooden cover rotted. No one comes out this way much."

"How did you find me?"

"Well, I started thinking that I should have a look around before I go to the police barracks to file my report. I figured that maybe I'd find some evidence that might be useful. I was walking in a large circle from where Anna was attacked, when I heard a strange noise. It took me a while to discover that it was coming from the well. Being under the ground muffles the sound quite a bit."

Heather carefully made her way to the edge of the hole and looked down.

"From here it looks like such a short distance to where I was. Only an arm's reach. But when you're down there . . ." she shivered.

"I know," said Michael, putting his arm around her. "How did you happen to come out here?"

Heather told him about the conversation she had overheard and about following the path.

"Do you have any idea who you heard talking?"

She shook her head. "But aren't Jack and Lloyd the only other men here, and Caroline, Mrs. Maxwell and Anna the only women?"

"Yes. But anyone could have parked out on the road and come across the fields without being noticed."

Heather smiled grimly. "That doesn't do much to narrow down the list of suspects."

"Don't worry about it now. Let's get you back to the house where you can sit down and rest. Are you sure that you're all right? Would you like a doctor?"

"I'm fine. And I've got a room to paint."

He laughed. "You don't have to prove how tough you are. Why not take the day off and go home? We'll forget about having you stay here tonight."

Heather was half inclined to agree, when the picture flashed through her mind of a face staring down at her from the top of the well; the face of someone who had disappeared without offering her help. Who would do that? she wondered. Suddenly finding out who was threatening Caroline was very personal to her. She wasn't certain enough of seeing the face to tell Michael, but she needed to find out.

"No. Why don't we stick with our original plan? After all, what happened to me was a genuine accident," said Heather. "Why don't you go make a report to the police and I'll get back to painting? It will be the best medicine for me."

"If you're sure," Michael said, looking doubtful as they walked back to the house.

The look of genuine concern on his face made her reach up and give him a quick kiss on the lips.

"Thanks for rescuing me," she said.

"Any time, if that's my reward."

"That's the second time in two days that you've kept me from falling."

"And the second kiss I've gotten. And this one was given much more graciously than last night in the parking lot, I must say," Michael said with a grin. "After you kissed me then, I thought you were going to follow it up with a right cross."

"I thought you kissed me," Heather replied.

"Hmm. Why don't we save that discussion until this evening? I think the matter of who is kissing whom is something that can only be worked out by means of careful experimentation."

They had reached the front of the house where Michael's car was parked. A man in his fifties came out of the front door, followed by George Webster. George waved to Michael and Heather. The other man got into a dark blue sedan and drove off as George returned to the house.

"Who is that?" asked Heather, noting that this added two more men to her list of potential voices.

"Thornton Jennings, he's George and Caroline's lawyer. They have him looking into Uncle Leo's will to see if there's a way of breaking it, so Caroline won't have to live in the house at night to meet the residency requirement."

"Any chance of that?"

Michael stopped by his car and shrugged. "Where there's a smart, ambitious lawyer there's always a way, but so far no luck."

"I'll see you later," Heather said, turning to enter the house. He took her arm and turned her towards him. He gave her a slow, lingering kiss. Heather's eyes opened wide in surprise, and she felt her heart skip a beat.

"What was that for?" she gasped.

"That's my down payment on the next time I have to rescue you."

"You don't have to rescue me to get a kiss," she said softly.

Michael smiled. "That's the first piece of good news I've had all day."

## Chapter Six

For the rest of the morning, Heather painted without incident. Her legs were stiff and sore from the fall at the well, so she was careful to plant her feet firmly on the rungs of the ladder. Even worse were her fingertips, raw from clinging to the stones. Fortunately she was able to find a pair of old gardening gloves in the back of the van. That made holding the brush more bearable. All these discomforts were easier to take as she watched the blue paint replace the white primer. Heather smiled to herself. It was like seeing the sun rise and replace the misty white of dawn with the richer tones of full daylight.

At the end of two hours of solid work, she got down from the ladder and admired the one long wall that she had finished. The transformation was amazing. The before and after difference was like seeing the ocean on a cloudy day and then when it's bathed in bright sunlight.

"That's mighty nice, Miss."

Heather spun around. Lloyd was standing in the doorway with a smile on his face.

"Sorry if I frightened you," he said, unconvincingly.

"You didn't frighten me. And I'm glad you like the work so far."

"I surely do. I guess I shouldn't be surprised that a pretty girl like yourself would do pretty work," he said, coming over to stand beside her.

Heather took a step away.

Lloyd grinned. "I can remember when this old place was quite something. Yes, indeed."

"Have you worked here long?"

"Over thirty years. Ever since Leo Compton took over the house after his father died. 'Course, even then the house had started to go downhill a bit. Reginald Compton was kind of tight with a dollar, especially after his wife Sarah died, but he was a regular big spender compared to his son. As long as the house kept a roof over his head until he died, that was all Leo cared about. Why, I used to bring up some plants myself that I got cheap at the end of the season and put them in the garden just to keep things looking halfway right."

"I can see why he kept you on as a gardener. You did more than you had to."

"Yeah, that was kind of a joke with Leo. He said that he couldn't pay me much, so he'd give me a big title. He used to call me his estate manager. I never understood exactly what that meant at the time."

"And I guess Mrs. Webster is still keeping you on as gardener?" asked Heather.

"Doesn't have a choice. That's part of the Compton will. She can't fire anyone who worked here when Leo died, at least not for three months. After that it's up to her, if she lasts out the three months, that is," Lloyd said, giving Heather a knowing look.

"You don't think she will?"

The man shrugged. "Heard you took a tumble down the old well today. That's a dangerous spot. I asked Leo to get me a new cover to put over it. That was over three years ago. He said that nobody was supposed to be out there who didn't know to watch out for it."

"It was too bad about what happened to Anna," said Heather, wondering if Lloyd's comment was meant as some kind of warning to her.

"A nasty piece of work, that one is. Probably a long line of fellas would like to scare the stuffing out of her. She always treated me like I was some kind of peasant."

"Who do you think is doing these things?"

"What things, Miss?"

"Smashing the mailbox and scaring Anna." Heather wanted to add the broken mirror and blood on the dresser, but didn't know if Michael had told Lloyd about those incidents.

"That's only two. Things happen sometimes. It doesn't mean they're fitted together." Lloyd went back to admiring the painted wall. "Yes, indeed, if they let you do the whole house, it would be a beautiful thing."

"Maybe Mrs. Webster will hire me to do more of the house. You never know."

Lloyd nodded, and walked back to the door. Then he turned and gave Heather a long look.

"There's something about Caroline Webster that reminds me of her Uncle Leo," he said. "A sort of blindness to what's around her. Now you, on the other hand," he gave her a slow wink. "You remind me of Sarah Compton. She was a fine woman. Had a real artistic side to her. I remember her from when I was just a boy."

"Was she Reginald's wife?"

"Yep. Michael and Caroline's grandmother." Lloyd gave a long sigh. "Well, it's not up to me to decide what happens here, I guess. I'm just the gardener."

Heather watched the old man shuffle down the hall and turn left toward the back of the house. She shivered. Time to get out of here for a while, she decided.

By the time Heather drove back to her apartment she was feeling stiff and tired. She wolfed down a peanut butter sandwich and swallowed a couple of aspirin with a glass of orange juice. She went through her closet, selecting a few items that would be appropriate for her stay at the Compton House. Should I take things suited for a formal dinner or for falling down a well? she asked herself. When she laughed out loud at her own humor, Heather realized that maybe she was a little overtired and should take a nap before making the return trip. She lay down on the sofa and pulled a quilt over herself, intending to rest for fifteen minutes.

When the phone rang, she immediately looked at her watch and realized that an hour had already passed.

"Hello," she said, wondering if it was someone from the Compton house trying to find out where she had disappeared to.

"Heather?" her mother asked. "Is everything all right?"

"I'm fine. Why?"

"You sounded strange."

"I was taking a nap."

"I thought you were working at the Compton House. I only called you on the off-chance that you might be home."

Heather debated how much to tell her mother, but decided that she couldn't hide the fact that she'd be away for a couple of nights. "I'm going to be staying at the Compton House for the next two nights or so. I came home to pick up some things."

"Staying there?"

"Yes. Their maid quit, and Caroline Webster would like some company. It's a big, old house you know."

"I thought you told me that her brother Michael was staying there."

"He'll be there too."

Her mother was silent for a moment. It wasn't like her mother to offer advice about men, so Heather wondered what was on her mind.

"I never liked that house; there was always a darkness about it."

"That can be changed: a little paint, some new wall-paper."

Her mother laughed. "That's not what I mean. And I know you're making fun of my rather mysterious way of talking about the place. I'll admit I do sound a bit like a fortune-teller at a traveling carnival, but Reginald Compton was a cold man. And his son Alex. Well, he positively gave me the shivers."

"Michael is Anthony's son, and you certainly got along with Anthony. Right?"

"Yes. As I've already told you, he recommended my work."

"Michael would probably like your work, too. In fact, he's a curator at The Boston Museum, and they've already purchased a couple of pieces of yours."

"Yes. Well . . . there is that, I suppose. I could ask around and see what people in the trade think of Michael Compton."

"No, Mother!" Heather said, rather more sharply than she intended. "People in the art world are great gossips. If you start asking around, it will get back to him, and I don't want that to happen."

"Because of the job?"

"Of course."

Heather could tell that somehow her mother had intuited that there was more to it than that.

"You know I make a point of staying out of your personal life. It's just this business with the Comptons. It worries me."

"I know it does," Heather said soothingly. "But don't be concerned. Remember, you painted that picture almost thirty-five years ago. Maybe the atmosphere has changed since then. By the way, what do you know about Reginald's wife, Sarah?"

"Not much. She died a number of years before I was at the house. Some of the servants suggested to me that she'd been the life of the place and had even made Reginald a tolerable human being. If you want an idea of what she looked like, there's a portrait of her at the top of the stairs on the second floor—or at least there was all those years ago. Not a first-rate work, in my opinion, but probably good enough to capture some simple likeness. Why do you ask?"

"Oh, I'd heard some interesting things about her. That's all."

"Hmm. I guess I'll let you go now. Are you leaving soon to go to the Comptons?"

"In a few minutes."

There was a long pause which was uncharacteristic for her mother, who would usually talk nonstop and then hang up abruptly.

"Be careful, Heather," her mother said in almost a

whisper. "Even if you think I'm being silly, would you at least take care?"

"Yes . . . yes, of course I will."

The line went dead and Heather sat on the sofa staring at the receiver. For the first time she actually felt apprehensive about returning to the house. Even the incident at the well had left her more angry than afraid, and the chance to spend more time with Michael had overshadowed any other concerns. But now, suddenly, she felt the bite of fear in her mind.

"Pull yourself together, girl," Heather said to herself. "You're scaring yourself by sitting home in the middle of a beautiful day when you should be out earning a living." Hoping to cheer herself, she punched in Abby's cell phone number. Heather wanted to tell her she'd be away, and fill her in on what had happened at the house. Abby's bracing wit would chase the cobwebs away.

Abby's phone was turned off. Heather smiled to herself. Abby always said you can reach me any time, just call on the cell phone. But half the time she had it turned off. Heather called Abby's home number and left a short message on her machine telling where she'd be that night and promising to give Abby a call that evening.

Picking up her small suitcase, she stood by the doorway for a moment looking back at her apartment, reluctant to leave.

"I'll be back," she said out loud, as if reassuring an audience of concerned friends. Then she shut the door.

"Back for more punishment," Jack said, as Heather walked into the front foyer.

She gave him a quizzical look.

"I heard about your falling into the well," he shook his head. "I told Lloyd we had to do something about that. I almost fell through myself when I first started to work here."

"Is that on the way to where you live?"

"Yeah. You go down the path to the left of the well and there's the stable."

"I guess that was too far away from the house to hear anything last night when Anna was attacked."

"Yeah, but to be honest, I probably had my headset on and was listening to music anyway, so I wouldn't have heard her even if she was right next door." He took Heather's suitcase from her hand. "Mrs. Maxwell said that I should show you where you'll be staying tonight. It's Anna's old room, but I guess they changed the sheets on the bed and everything."

As they reached the top of the staircase, Heather made a point of noticing if there was still a portrait of Sarah Compton at the head of the stairs. It was still there though the location was so dark, due to the heavy draperies covering the windows above the staircase, that one could easily have thought from a distance that the portrait was merely a rectangular shadow.

The young woman in the picture was dressed in an off-the-shoulder evening gown that looked to be from the 1920s. Although not conventionally pretty, there was an intelligence and humor in the face that suggested she would have been an interesting person to know. She doesn't look the least bit like me, Heather thought, but I think we could have been friends.

"She's one of the family," Jack said, coming back to stand by her side. "I think Lloyd said that it's Sarah. She was the wife of the one who owned the house before Leo. I guess this whole hall used to be filled with paintings of their family going back to who knows when. At least that's what Lloyd says."

"Where are the paintings now?" Heather asked. It might be interesting to see the one her mother painted if it was still hanging somewhere.

"I think Leo had them all stored up in the attic."

"I wonder why?"

Jack shrugged and headed down the hall. "Leo got a little funny toward the end. He couldn't see very well, maybe he thought the eyes were following him. Or maybe he thought the family was pretty ugly. Although I guess you might think Michael isn't too bad," he added, giving her a wink."

Heather replied with a neutral smile. So much for their date being a secret.

Jack threw open a door about halfway down the hall. "Here it is!" he announced.

Heather went inside. The room seemed almost as large as her entire apartment, although it may only have seemed so because it was almost completely devoid of furniture. True, there was a double bed on one wall and a dresser with a mirror on the wall opposite, but aside from a severe wooden chair in the far corner, the room was empty. This allowed you to see vast expanses of the dingy striped wall paper. Put prison bars on the windows and it would have all the charm of a solitary-confinement cell, Heather thought. She pushed the switch next to the door and a dull yellow light came from the aging fixture in the center of the ceiling. It threw just enough light to make you wonder what you weren't seeing.

"Anna used to sneak furniture in from the room next door, but Mrs. Maxwell had me put it all back. But you can look around in there later. If you see anything you like, give me a call and I'll move it in here for you."

"I don't expect to be staying that long," Heather said, thinking that one night might seem an eternity.

"You never know," Jack said, giving her another wink.

Heather spent the remainder of the afternoon unpacking her things and finding the huge but antiquated bathroom back near the stairwell. She also took Jack's advice and investigated the room next door. This space was apparently being used as a storage room and was haphazardly filled with small tables, lamps, stuffed chairs, and several ornate mirrors.

Deciding to be comfortable even if she stayed only two nights, Heather dragged over a reasonably suitable stuffed chair that exuded only the faintest odor of mildew when she sat down in it. Probably it would be quite nice if it were reupholstered, she guessed. She found one of the two electric plugs in the room and put the chair next to it along with an end table and a small glass lamp. At least she'd be able to read at night. When she stood back and gazed at her assemblage, she smiled and decided that the best you could call it was Victorian eclectic.

Although it was late in the afternoon by now, Heather decided to go downstairs to the dining room to see how the new blue paint looked in the late afternoon. Since no one seemed to be around, Heather thought that this might be a good time to catch up on what she hadn't gotten done that afternoon while she spent time at home. Perhaps she could at least paint the short wall in the front with the bay window. She stopped in the doorway to study the wall that had been completed. Even in the late afternoon with the sun slanting through the front window onto the dusty oak floor, there was still a glow from the blue wall that seemed to diffuse throughout the room.

As she walked closer, checking for any imperfections, the sun seemed to linger over a particularly white spot on the wall near the back wall. As Heather drew nearer, she saw that this was not a trick of the light.

'GET OUT' had been scrawled in white primer over her newly painted blue wall. Heather took a step back as if she had been struck. She reached out with a shaking hand to touch the letters. It was still wet! Someone had done this since she had returned to the house this afternoon. Heather looked around quickly to see if anyone was nearby waiting to see her reaction. The room was empty.

Heather took a deep breath, more angry than afraid. That someone would deface her work in order to frighten her away from the Compton House made her want to fight all the harder to find out who was behind this vandalism. This attack on her work brought out all the stubbornness that she relied upon to make a success of her business. She wasn't about to let the coward who was trying to terrorize her get away with costing her an important job.

She went over to her supplies and picked up a rag. Since the primer was still wet, much of it came off with a little rubbing. Heather then opened the can of blue paint. Using a light touch with a sponge applicator, she carefully blended out the letters. Fifteen minutes later she stood back, deciding that the words now only existed in her imagination. Since she already had the can of blue paint opened, Heather moved her ladder over to the back wall and continued working.

Heather lost all sense of time as she worked and noticed only in passing the shifting angle of the late spring sunlight. When she had first started to work, the wall had been shrouded in shadows, but now as the late afternoon sun came pouring through the western bay window in the front of the house, the eastern wall she was working on came alive. Every turn of her roller bathed the wall in a mix of blue sky and sea.

"Miss?" a timid voice asked.

Heather looked down, and saw Mrs. Maxwell standing at the foot of her ladder. I really should focus better on what's going on around me, Heather thought. Somebody could knock me off this ladder, and I wouldn't know it until I hit the ground.

"How do you like it?" she asked the cook.

"Very nice," the woman said politely. "Mrs. Webster called earlier and said that she won't be back until after dinner. She's visiting some friends in Worcester. And Mr. Webster just called and said that he's been delayed in Boston and won't be here for dinner. Would you like to have your dinner on a tray in the front parlor?"

What was Michael doing in Boston? Heather thought with growing irritation. He hadn't mentioned that trip to me. Probably visiting his fiancée. I do him a favor by staying in the house, and now I'm completely abandoned.

"It is the only fully furnished room on this floor," Mrs. Maxwell added.

"Excuse me," Heather said, having lost track of the conversation.

"The front parlor is probably the best place to eat because it's fully furnished. Mr. Leo usually ate in there. I can have Jack lay a fire in the fireplace. The furnace has been turned off for the season."

"That will be swell," she said to Mrs. Maxwell.

Just swell, she thought to herself.

## Chapter Seven

"Things went better than I ever expected they would," Heather said to herself, stretching out her tired legs.

Mrs. Maxwell was a good cook and had served a fine roast beef dinner with lots of fresh vegetables. The raspberry torte she presented for dessert made Heather wish that she had a place to keep a cook in her apartment, not to mention the money to pay one. A large end table with a beautiful burled rosewood top had served as her dinner table, and Mrs. Maxwell had carefully covered it with a thick white tablecloth.

Now Heather was sitting on a loveseat, drinking hot chocolate, and reading a book on early twentieth century design that she'd found on the shelf. Sarah Compton's name was written inside. Occasionally Heather found herself dreamily staring into the fire.

She felt relaxed, and, she realized, quite at home. It wasn't the extravagance of being waited on, she thought, but the gentle comfort of the house itself surrounding her. The soft patina of the wood, the stone carvings above the fireplace mantle, even the slightly threadbare carpeting of Persian design. Somehow it all fit together in a soothing harmony that enveloped her in a warm restfulness. The past lives that had been lived in the house seemed to reach out to include her in the continuity of the generations. She felt at peace, an integral part of something larger than herself. Heather set down her cup of chocolate and her eyes closed as she began to drift off.

Someone sat down on the other end of the love seat.

Heather's eyes flew open.

"Sorry if I frightened you," Michael said softly, reaching over to kiss her softly on the cheek. "I see you've managed to settle in okay."

"Pretty well, under the circumstances," she replied quickly, then regretted having sounded so irritable.

"I know. I apologize for not being here for dinner. I had to finish up a project that I was working on at the museum."

"I thought you were on leave?"

"Yes. Well, this was an exhibition that I had convinced the museum to take on, so I felt responsible to see that it got set up properly."

"Ah," Heather said, thinking that he certainly looked sincere. But there was something, maybe a slight excess of solemnity about the whole thing that suggested there was more to this than met the eye. "What sort of show is it?"

"Sculpture. Welded metal. That sort of thing. Not everyone's cup of tea."

"Is it yours?"

He shrugged. "I suppose I like to think that I can appreciate innovations in art even if I don't particularly like them. If that makes any sense."

Heather nodded, tired of the topic. She wanted to ask if he had managed to fit in a date with his fiancée.

"Did anything happen around here today?" Michael asked, as if reading her mind and taking an evasive maneuver.

Heather told him about the graffiti on the wall. He stared into the fire for a moment.

"I think I made a mistake asking you to stay. Apparently all that's done is turn you into a target. You should leave. Perhaps the repainting of the dining room should even be postponed until we get this matter settled."

Heather shook her head. "Before we do anything as drastic as that, let's think this thing through. Why would anyone be making life so difficult for you and your sister?"

"People in the town don't like us. They're harassing us in order to get the last of the Comptons to leave town," he suggested.

"Do you actually know of anyone in town who dislikes your family that much?"

"No. I'm just going by what I've heard. I don't know the people around here, and like I told you last night, the state police don't really know the locals either. But what other reason could there be?"

"It just seems to me that somebody is going to an awful lot of trouble and risk to drive Caroline out of town. I mean somebody had to walk right into the dining room to write that message on the wall."

"Was the front door locked when you came back from lunch?"

Heather shook her head.

"You see. That's the way it always is. Somebody locks up at night and opens the door in the morning. Anyone could waltz in any time in between, then hide in one of the empty rooms until they saw their opportunity. Especially with Anna gone, there's no one keeping track of what happens in the front of the house."

"Let's keep the door locked, then," Heather said. "At least we can make it hard for this vandal. If we're not going to fight, then we may as well give up and leave."

Michael frowned. "That may be happening sooner than you think. That business with Anna last night has shaken Caroline. That's why she had the lawyer here today. Unless there is some way that she can stay out of the house at night, she's talking about forgetting the whole thing and letting the estate go to charity. He promised to have a final answer for her by tomorrow, but I don't hold out much hope for getting around the terms of Leo's will."

"But then the house will probably be torn down, the land sold, and some kind of development will go up," Heather said. Even though she had only been in the house for two days, that seemed almost too much to bear.

"I don't want to see the house torn down, either. But I can't fix it up, and even if I could, it's too far to commute from here to Boston."

The mention of Boston reminded Heather that she still had a question to ask.

"When you were in Boston did you happen to see . . ." she began, trying to casually open up the topic of his fiancée.

"Hello all!" Caroline bellowed from the doorway.

She stood there leaning with her hands on either side of the door-frame surveying the room as if a party was going on and she was looking for a familiar face. Finally she walked across the room and stood directly in front of Heather.

"Nice of you to stay here with me," she said, sticking out her hand.

Heather shook it and noticed that Caroline's eyes had the glittery look of someone whose dinner had included more alcohol than was good for her.

"Thank you for having me," Heather replied.

Caroline gave a nod, then carefully made her way across the room to collapse in the wing chair next to the fire.

"I had a wonderful evening. You know who was there, Michael?"

"Who?" he asked, glancing apologetically at Heather.

"Birdie."

"Who?"

"Barbara Birdwell. You must remember Birdie. We went to school together. She came over to the house lots of times when Mum and Dad were alive."

"I seem to remember her."

"Of course you do," insisted Caroline. "She's so funny. She can keep you in stitches for hours."

Caroline then went on to recount a long, disconnected story which quickly became incomprehensible. Heather nodded and smiled in what seemed to be the right places, but soon realized that Caroline was oblivious to what was going on around her. She was merely reciting events and had no need of an encouraging audience. The fire had died down a bit, and since Heather had worn a skirt, thinking that the occasion called for a bit of formality, her legs were cold. She curled them up under her. Seeing what she was doing, Michael opened a trunk at the other end of the love seat and took out a knitted afghan. He carefully spread it over her lap, then sat down again close to her on the love seat.

"Mrs. Maxwell showed me where that was last night," he whispered.

As Caroline's endless story droned on, Heather found her eyes starting to close again. Her chin had almost reached her chest before she awoke with a start. Something had touched her foot. She was about to jump up with a cry of 'Rat!' when she realized that what was touching her foot under the afghan was most definitely a human hand.

She glanced over at Michael. He refused to meet her eye but she detected a hint of mischief around his mouth. He stared steadfastly forward as though what Birdie had to say about why Broadway shows weren't what they used to be was fascinating stuff. The hand slowly made its way up to her ankle. Heather realized that she was holding her breath and let it out with such a gasp that even Caroline paused for a moment as if wondering whether she had heard a gust of wind. After she resumed her story, the hand slowly crept up to her calf.

I should slap his hand away, thought Heather, or at least get up and move. He leaves me alone half the evening and then comes back and expects to fool around. But she felt as though all the bones in her body had dissolved and the muscles had turned to porridge. She couldn't have stirred from that spot on the love seat if her life depended on it. Slowly the hand crept up to right behind her knee. It tickled at first and she was afraid she was going to giggle. Even Caroline would notice if she broke into a fit of hysterical laughter, unless it happened to coincide with one of Birdie's witticisms. But then Heather didn't want to giggle any more as the hand moved up to where the hem of skirt was pulled tightly into the back of her legs.

"And then the frog jumped!" Caroline shouted triumphantly. She leaped from her chair as if it were electrified and came over to stand in front of Michael and Heather.

The hand disappeared as Heather sat bolt upright in surprise.

"So what do you think of that?" Caroline said, staring down at Heather.

"Amazing! Absolutely amazing!" Heather said with heartfelt agreement.

"Birdie thought so, too," said Caroline.

For once Heather found herself in agreement with Birdie.

"I think it's time for me to go off to bed," Caroline said, giving a large yawn and suddenly looking tired. She slowly wandered toward the hall.

"Would you see her up to her room?" Michael asked softly. His eyes still had a glimmer of mischief but his face was serious. "I'm going to lock the doors and make sure all the windows are secured."

Heather nodded.

Michael smiled. "And although I'd rather not have to say this for several reasons, make sure you lock yourself in tonight. Okay?"

"Don't worry. For several reasons I will."

Caroline seemed to sober up considerably on the walk up the stairs. But Heather accompanied her to her room anyway, turned on the light and took a quick look around just in case.

"Thanks again," Caroline said, impulsively throwing her arms around a surprised Heather and giving her a hug. "I didn't think I could spend another night in this house, but Birdie told me not to be a quitter. 'You never quit in field hockey, Compton,' she said, 'and you can't quit now.' That's what she told me."

Heather smiled and nodded. "If you need me in the night, I'm three doors up the hall in Anna's old room. Just knock," she said, touched by the woman's affection.

Once back in her room, after a visit to the bathroom, Heather realized that there was no key in the lock of her door. Probably Anna misplaced it somewhere, Heather thought. Not wanting to disturb Caroline or go searching for Michael, she dragged her reading chair in front of the door, feeling a bit silly about such precautions. Caroline is the one they want out of the house, Heather thought, not me. But of course frightening off the help like Anna and myself could be part of their plan. Deciding that it was better to be safe than sorry, she shoved the chair hard against the door.

She moved the end table to the side of her bed and stretched the lamp cord until it just reached the table. At least this way she could turn on a light if necessary. Heather climbed into the high bed and finally got comfortable, or at least as comfortable as she could get, given the rather dramatic sag in the middle of the mattress. Probably a number of Comptons have been born and died in this bed, she thought grimly. The first thing she would do if she were Caroline was to replace all the mattresses and box springs. Since it was only going on eleven, she reached into her bag on the floor next to the bed, pulled out her cell phone, and punched the button for Abby's home number.

"Hello," a sleepy voice finally answered.

"Is that you, Abby?"

"Who wants to know?"

"It's Heather."

"Yeah, well this is Michelangelo, the guy who spent half the day on her back painting the ceilings in the Burger Hut johns. The guy who's going to need a chiropractor to get out of bed in the morning."

"Tough work?" Heather said sympathetically.

"That doesn't begin to describe it. By the time the manager showed up and we dithered around over colors, it was almost noon. I've still got a day's work to do there tomorrow. I never met a fast food manager who worried more about the decor in the restrooms than about the food. I think I might be in love. He's really something special." Abby paused. "Talking about special, what are you doing staying out at the Compton House?"

Heather recounted the day's events to Abby, starting with Michael's request that she stay there, and covering the well experience and the threat written on the wall.

"Quite a day, huh?" she concluded lightly, expecting Abby to laugh. There was silence on the other end of the line.

"If that's a double bed you're sleeping in and if there isn't already someone on the other side, hold the spot for me; I can be there in forty-five minutes," Abby finally said. Her tone of voice told Heather that she wasn't joking.

"I'll be fine."

"Are you crazy? Just listen to yourself. Someone is willing to let you drown in a well, and you're telling me everything is okay."

"I thought I saw a face. I could have imagined it. Falling in the well was my own fault."

"Did you write 'Get Out' to yourself on the wall too?"

"That's really not much more than a prank."

"Like that maid getting mugged."

"She wasn't hurt, and lots of people didn't like her."

There was a grunt on the other end of the line. "It could be that lots of people don't like you either. You know, I'm usually the one who does crazy things, but since you started working in that house, it's like you've been hypnotized. All sorts of weird stuff is happening around you, and all you can think about is whether that blue paint will look just right in the dining room."

There was enough truth in what Abby said to make Heather pause. She wasn't acting like her usual sensible self. The Compton House and Michael had woven a spell that made her willing to take a chance, a chance bigger than any she'd taken since Richard had walked out of her life over two years ago. But how much was she willing to risk? How far should she go?

"Heather?"

"Yes."

"I thought a ghost had gotten you there for a moment."

"I was just thinking. Look, I'll be fine tonight. Let's see how things go tomorrow. If I get a full day in, I'll be able to finish the blue coat on the dining room, and you can complete those restrooms. We can talk about what to do next. Unless Caroline is certain she's going to stay, she might not want us to do the stenciling along the top. Of course that would be a shame, because I've had several ideas. You know, it would be nice . . ."

"Whoa! You were starting to make sense up until the end. Don't start thinking about stencils when the owner may be hitting the road in the next day or two," Abby warned. "I'll call you sometime tomorrow afternoon. I don't think you should spend another night out there alone. Maybe your friend Michael can shoo the ghosts out of a second room, and we'll both move in with our client. A whole new personal approach to painting."

"Okay, we can talk about it tomorrow."

"Yeah. Get some sleep. And don't go wandering around the halls of that castle at night."

"I won't."

"And if you hear any noises . . ."

"Yeah?"

"Roll over and go back to sleep."

## Chapter Eight

Heather didn't know how long she had been asleep. It seemed like her head had just hit the pillow. But when she looked at the illuminated dial of her watch on the table next to the bed, it showed two A.M. She rolled over, trying to get back to sleep quickly before the uncomfortable bed brought her fully awake. Then she heard it. A scraping sound. For a moment she dismissed it as the normal creaking of an old house, but then she had to admit that it was coming from the area of her door.

She switched on the light. The noise stopped, but the chair was definitely pushed out a few inches from the now closed door.

"Caroline?" she called out softly. A second later, "Michael?"

When there was no answer, she got out of bed and crept over to the doorway. She stood there listening. Nothing.

Suddenly the door flew open again and the chair jammed into her legs. Without thinking, she pushed back. The door closed several inches, then whoever was on the other side also began to push harder. Slowly Heather began to lose the contest and the chair gradually came toward her as her feet lost their grip on the smooth wood floor. She tried to crane her neck around the edge of the door to discover the identity of her attacker, but all she could make out was an arm covered in dark cloth.

"Help!" she cried out as loudly as she could.

She fell forward into the chair as the pressure on the other side instantly disappeared. She was half lying across the chair when there was a knock on her door.

"Heather?" Michael called.

She quickly slid the chair away from the door and pulled it open. He was wearing only a pair of gym shorts and carrying a baseball bat. She flung her arms around him and buried her face in his chest. His arms enfolded her.

"What happened?" he asked after a minute. Heather waited to speak until her breathing returned to normal, and she felt she could talk without gasping.

"Someone tried to push my door open," she said stepping back, realizing that her own shorts and T-shirt left little to the imagination.

"Why didn't you lock the door?"

"There was no key. Anna must have taken it with her or put it someplace. I had shoved a chair in front of the door, but it slid pretty easily on these wood floors."

"Did you see who it was?"

She shook her head.

"I'll be right back," Michael said. A moment later he returned and pressed a large key into her hand. "This is a skeleton key. It works in all the locks in the house. This way you can lock the door."

"How many people have one of these?" she asked.

Michael smiled. "I'd guess that the locks haven't been changed in over a hundred years, everyone within ten miles might have one for all I know. I realize that isn't very reassuring, but it's better than the chair solution."

Heather nodded. "Is Caroline okay?"

"I checked her door. It's locked. There's no point in waking her up just to tell her what's happened. I'll break it to her gently in the morning," Michael said. He pushed a wayward strand of hair from Heather's face, then smiled. "Try to get some sleep."

"I will. I'm sorry I didn't get to see who it was."

"I'm glad you didn't. Who knows what might have happened if you'd seen the person." He reached out and stroked her cheek. "I'm going to check the house over."

"Be careful."

"Whoever it was no doubt is long gone. You scared the guy off."

"Well, the guy scared me pretty good, too. I'd say we're even."

Michael looked at her for a moment, then shook his head. "You're pretty amazing."

"Why?"

"By day you paint the house, and by night you defend it." He gave her a careful once-over. "And you look pretty good, too."

Heather blushed. "See you in the morning," she said, starting to close the door.

"Uh, I think I'll get a chair and sit out here by your door once I'm done checking the house. Just in case our friend comes back."

After she locked the door and turned out the light,

Heather thought she would lie awake for hours listening for an intruder. However, the thought that Michael was right outside the door comforted her. After a few images of Michael looking long and lean in his gym shorts and picturing the affection in his eyes as he'd looked at her, Heather fell asleep.

She got up once in the night and stepped out in the hall. Sure enough, right outside her door Michael sat in jeans and a sweatshirt. He was sound asleep, but the baseball bat rested across his knees, as ready for action as the sword of any knight of the round table. Heather got an extra blanket from her room, and being careful not to disturb him, she gently placed it over the sleeping man. Pausing to smile at the relaxed, almost boyish expression, on his handsome face, she realized that although it was nice to be independent, there were also times when relying on someone else could be a comfort.

"Good morning," Jack said the next morning, looking up from a plate of bacon and eggs. "How'd you sleep?"

"Fine," Heather replied.

She wasn't sure whether to keep last night's incident a secret. Michael had been gone when she left her room this morning, leaving only the empty chair as evidence that last night's adventure hadn't been a dream. She decided to err on the side of discretion.

Mrs. Maxwell came into the kitchen. "Mrs. Webster is feeling a bit under the weather this morning and will be eating in her bedroom. Would you like to eat in the front parlor again?"

"No. It's past eight, and I really should get to work," Heather replied. "If you could just bring me a glass of juice, a piece of toast and some coffee, I'll get right to work in the dining room."

"Lloyd just pulled up out back," she said to Jack, who quickly wiped his mouth with a napkin and stood.

"We're going to try sealing that well today. A little bit like locking the barn door after the cow has gotten out, but at least there won't be any more accidents." He paused for a second. "I guess that came out wrong."

"I got your point," said Heather, grinning.

"And there's a window to repair. Michael told me this morning just before he left that he found a broken window in the dining room when he was checking around last night. Did you see it yesterday?"

Heather shook her head.

"A pane in the back window, he said. I'll go to the hardware store this afternoon and get a piece of glass cut to fit it. I should have it fixed before tonight." He waved to Heather and Mrs. Maxwell, then headed out the back door.

"Did Mr. Webster say where he was going when he left this morning?" Heather asked.

Mrs. Maxwell hesitated as if not sure how much she should tell about her employer's whereabouts.

"I believe he was going to Boston."

"I see," Heather said.

Heather walked down the hall to the foyer, then turned left toward the dining room. From the amount of light shining in through the hall windows, it was clearly going to be another sunny day. Good for seeing the true colors while painting, she thought. Before checking her equipment, Heather immediately went to the back window to examine the break.

They were old casement windows. They opened outward and had a handle on the inside that turned down to lock them closed. Someone had broken the pane right next to the handle which would have enabled him to get inside. Heather opened the window and leaned out, examining the ground. Maybe a trained police officer could find something by searching for footprints, but all Heather could tell was that it would be easy for anyone of normal height to climb from ground level through the window. Glass inside on the floor showed that the window had been broken from the outside.

Heather sighed. I guess Michael was right, she thought, it must be someone in town who has it in for the Comptons.

Heather maneuvered her ladder to the inside wall and went to work. She had completed the section along the molding and was bending over a can of paint getting ready to pour it into her roller tray, when she heard the clicking of women's shoes coming down the hall. She glanced up expecting to see Caroline enter the room, but it was a woman of about her own age, wearing jeans and a dark red tank top that went well with her jet black hair, although Heather thought it was a bit chilly for such an outfit. As the person came closer, Heather could see that the woman was as tall as she was, but the newcomer had a two-inch advantage due to her high heels. Her bare shoulders and arms had the clearly defined muscles that Heather associated with an athlete, and she walked toward Heather with a catlike grace.

When the woman was a few feet from Heather, she flashed perfect white teeth.

"Sorry to bother you, but no one answered the door so I just walked inside. I figured I would just wander around until I found someone."

Heather smiled back ruefully. "Security isn't the best around here."

"But it is a wonderful house, isn't it?" the woman said,

looking around as if delighted with what she had just found.

Heather agreed. "I think Mrs. Webster is around some- where, but she wasn't feeling well earlier. I can have the cook look for her if you want."

The woman shook her head. "Actually, I was looking for Michael Compton. I'm his fiancée."

When Heather recounted this meeting to Abby over the phone at lunch time, she swore that she hadn't even blinked on hearing this bit of information.

Abby was doubtful. "Maybe you think you looked like the sphinx, but I'll bet this woman thought you were about to go into cardiac arrest. Or that you had just dis- covered that your tongue had turned into a frog."

"Nope. I was the perfect lady. She told me her name was Renata Sisco. I smiled and told her that I was Heather Martinson and that Michael was probably in Boston."

"And is that when she told you that Michael was prob- ably busy in Boston putting the finishing touches on an exhibition of her sculpture at the museum?" asked Abby.

"Yeah. It turns out she didn't get those muscles in the gym but by welding big chunks of scrap metal into so- called art."

"Temper, temper," Abby warned.

"Sorry. Well, anyway she drove all the way out to see Michael. Something about the exhibit, she claimed, and he had gone in to Boston, probably to see her. She laughed and said it seemed 'very O'Henry'. "

"My, my. And you didn't hit her?"

"You didn't see her muscles."

Abby was silent for a moment. "Seriously, what are

you going to do? If you really like this guy, you've got a problem."

"I just don't understand. He seems so nice, I find it hard to believe that he would be so sweet to me if he had this gorgeous, talented fiancée in Boston. I guess I'm going to have to confront him as soon as he gets back."

"Right. No sense having you protect his sister when he could have the queen of the junk yard doing it," said Abby. "So did she leave when she found out Michael wasn't there?"

"She took off without even waiting to see if Caroline was available," said Heather. "The whole thing seemed a little odd. Why drive all the way out here without checking to see if Michael was going to be around?"

"Maybe they're not the closest couple in the world of art. How about the other stuff, no more threats or anything?"

Heather gave her a brief account of the door pushing incident, leaving out the details of how Michael had looked in his gym shorts.

"Good lord, Heather, have you checked in the basement of that place for a coffin filled with good Transylvanian earth?"

"How are the rest rooms coming?" asked Heather, changing the subject.

"Now Jim wants me to paint little hamburger people at different points around the room. That's going to take forever."

"Who's Jim?"

"The manager."

"Sounds like the two of you are getting kind of friendly."

"Well . . . he did ask me out tonight. But I said I had to come out to be with you."

Heather paused. "Look, it sounds like you've still got a lot of work to do there. Why not keep your date with Jim? Otherwise you'll have a long trip back and forth tomorrow."

"I want to give you a hand. It sounds bad out there," Abby insisted.

"I don't think there's much you can do right now. Anyway, I may be home tonight if Michael doesn't have some good answers."

"If you're sure . . ."

"Yeah. I'll give you a call late tonight."

"It's a first date. I won't be out very late."

"That's what you always say."

## Chapter Nine

The afternoon went by quietly, and Heather completed the other long wall. She had saved the front wall until last because that was the one that Uncle Leo had begun to paint. The primer hadn't concealed his shade of deep blue as well as it covered the decades-old pale peach. She suspected that she might have to give that wall two coats. Heather had just pulled her ladder around to the front wall when Caroline Webster entered the room. She was wearing a dark-green mohair sweater and black slacks. A bit cheerless for a spring day, but certainly demonstrating, once again, her love of green.

"You're making great progress," she said, smiling somewhat hesitantly, as if she wasn't accustomed to being so enthusiastic around laborers.

"How do you like the color?" Heather asked, hoping that it was the friendly Caroline of last night she was facing and not the aloof person who had hired her.

Caroline walked into the center of the room and looked critically at the three completed walls.

"You know, I like it much better than I would have expected," she finally announced.

"Good," said Heather, deciding to take this as a rave review.

"We never did decide on that stenciling," Caroline said, "I was wondering . . . ," she walked closer to the walls and stared up at the molding. "What would you think about having a pattern that was eighteen inches wide?"

A foot was the widest that she'd ever done. Eighteen inches would be awfully wide, Heather began to say, but then chose to be more diplomatic.

"It's hard to judge without having a sense of what it would look like," Heather said. She walked over to her gear box and pulled out a tape measure. "Let's hold this up to the top of the wall and come down eighteen, then we can visualize how it would be."

"Okay," said Caroline. "Why don't we use the other ladder, since yours is already set up for painting?"

Heather nodded, and between the two of them they placed the second ladder up against the outside long wall.

"Why don't I go up first?" said Caroline, taking the tape measure out of Heather's hand. "I'd like to see what the room looks like from up there."

Heather stood at the bottom of the twelve-foot step ladder as Caroline went up. About half way up Caroline suddenly turned to look at Heather with a puzzled expression on her face. Before Heather could ask what was wrong, there was a cracking sound. With a scream, Caroline fell backwards into Heather. Heather tried to catch her, but the sudden impact was too much and she tumbled backwards onto the floor.

For a long moment, Heather lay there trying to catch her breath. Caroline had struck her hard in the midriff, knocking the wind out of her. She slowly propped herself up on one elbow. Caroline was sitting a few feet away holding her ankle, her face contorted in pain.

"How bad is it?" Heather asked.

"I think it's broken," Caroline snapped. "Go get Jack, he'll have to drive me to the hospital."

Heather got to her feet, leaning against the ladder for a second to get her balance.

"Quickly," Caroline insisted.

"Where is he?"

"Probably out by the stable well with Lloyd."

Weaving slightly from side to side, Heather made her way down the hall to the kitchen. Mrs. Maxwell was nowhere to be seen, but the door to her quarters off the kitchen were closed. Probably taking a midday nap, Heather thought briefly. She went out the back kitchen door and wandered randomly for a while until she found the trail that she had followed the other day. Fortunately, Caroline was right. As she came through the bushes, she could see Jack leaning on a shovel and listening patiently while Lloyd explained exactly how he wanted something done.

"Mrs. Webster's been hurt. She fell off the ladder."

"What was she doing on a ladder?" Lloyd asked.

Jack immediately ran past her heading toward the house.

Lloyd shook his head. "This is getting out of hand."

Not waiting to find out what Lloyd meant, Heather rushed to follow Jack to see if she could be of any help. By the time she got back to the dining room, he was kneeling over Caroline and asking her to try rotating her foot.

"I don't think it's broken," he said after a minute, "but you'll need an X-ray to be sure. "You probably have a sprain."

Caroline took in a ragged breath and nodded. "It's a wonder I'm not dead. How dare you bring defective equipment into my home?" she said to Heather. "You're responsible for this."

Heather's throat tightened and she didn't say anything.

"My lawyer is going to be here later on today. I'm going to take this matter up with him. Get me up," she barked at Jack.

Putting his arm around her, he lifted Caroline to her feet. She took a few tentative hops on her good foot while Jack supported her on the other side.

"Help me out to the foyer. I'll wait there while you bring the car around."

Heather watched them walk slowly out of the dining room and down the hall. She could hear Caroline telling Jack to call her husband immediately and complaining loudly that Michael was never here when you needed him.

Heather had to admit that she agreed. It would be nice to have Michael here once in a while when things started to go wrong. Immediately the memory of him coming to her rescue last night made her feel she was being unfair. But where was he? Probably back in Boston helping his stunning fiancée set up her pile of scrap metal.

At any rate, this ruins everything, she thought grimly, feeling tears start up at the back of her eyes. The job here is over. Heck, I'll be lucky if I don't get sued. How could that have happened? She walked over to the broken ladder and looked at the step. There was a small jagged piece of wood at one end where it had snapped; the rest of the step had broken off cleanly. She and Abby had used this ladder steadily for months; it had never given any sign of weakening. And Caroline Webster wasn't exactly a heavyweight.

"Pretty strange, huh?"

With a start she realized that Lloyd was standing next to her, looking at the ladder. He bent down and ran his hand over the broken step.

"What's strange?" she asked.

"That someone would cut through the step on your ladder like that."

"Cut!"

"Yep. Looks like whoever it was used a narrow blade, maybe a coping saw. They left just enough wood so the first person who stepped on it would break it off." He glanced up at her. "You're lucky. It was probably meant for you."

"Somebody meant to kill me?"

"Not kill," Lloyd corrected. "If you wanted to kill somebody this way, you'd cut one of the higher steps where they'd have farther to fall. This was just meant to give you a scare and maybe a broken leg at worst."

Great, she thought, who would mind a broken leg. "I wonder when it was done?"

Lloyd stood up with difficulty and shrugged. "Could have been anytime since you left this stuff here. Nobody's been keeping track of it."

It could have happened any time after the first day of work, because Abby had used the ladder then, Heather thought. Someone could have tampered with it yesterday when I went home for lunch or late in the afternoon when I was up in my room. It could even have been done last night by whoever broke in.

"Well, this ladder's no good to anybody. Do you want me to help you take it out to your van?"

"Thanks anyway, but we'd better leave it. The police might want to take a look at it. Would you be willing to tell Mrs. Webster that you think it was cut?"

"Sure." Lloyd grinned. "Although I haven't had a whole lot of luck telling her much of anything so far."

Promising that he'd try to catch Mrs. Webster before she left for the hospital, Lloyd ambled down the hall. With a sigh, Heather returned to the wall she'd been working on. If she was going to be fired that day, at least she would have completed painting the four walls. Putting her weight down extra hard on each step and bouncing a bit to check for any damage to the other ladder, Heather returned to work. It turned out that her estimate was correct. The wall Leo had worked on did require two coats of paint, so it was almost five o'clock when she got down from the ladder and looked over her completed job.

Even if this is all I do in this house, she told herself, gazing up and down the room, I can still say that I've made a big improvement. The moment of pride faded as she thought about how things might have been, getting to decorate more of the house, having the opportunity to spend more time with Michael . . . she shook the dreams away, and began gathering her gear together. She wasn't going to leave anything else sitting out to be vandalized.

She had just gotten the last of her things sorted and the van safely locked up when Jack pulled up in front of the house. He was alone.

"How did it go?" she asked.

"Well, there was quite a bit of moaning and groaning until the X-rays turned out negative and the doctor told her that it wasn't even that bad a sprain," Jack said with a smile, then suddenly his face turned worried. "The doctor said that she was lucky that she fell on you or she could have seriously hurt her back or head."

"Where is she? They didn't keep her in the hospital, did they?"

"Nah. Mr. Webster came out and picked her up. He wanted her to come back to Boston with him, but she insisted that she had to spend the night in the house. I think they were going somewhere for dinner."

"Did Lloyd get a chance to talk to her?"

Jack nodded. "Right before we left. Mrs. Webster didn't say much at first, I think she would rather believe that it was some defect in your ladder than vandalism. But I could see that she took it kind of seriously. The more she thought about it, the more worried she looked."

"She is going to come back here tonight, though, isn't she? She isn't giving up on taking over the house."

"Don't know. Mrs. Webster, her husband, and that lawyer are going to meet back here later on, as far as I could make out. Maybe they'll decide then. Are you going to stay here again tonight?"

"I'll have to talk that over with Michael whenever he comes back."

"Okay. Should I tell Mrs. Maxwell to set you up for dinner in the front parlor again?"

Heather paused. She didn't want Caroline and her husband to come back early and find her set up in the front room like one of the family.

"Do you think she would mind bringing something up to my room on a tray, or I can come get it in the kitchen? Tell her not to fuss."

Jack laughed. "I won't tell her that, she cooks for me, too. I'm sure she'll have something great all prepared, and I don't think she'll mind bringing it up to you."

When Jack left to go to the kitchen, Heather tried the doors on the van one last time to make sure they were all locked. Then she walked slowly back inside the great house. She had to admit that she was tired. More than tired, her body was feeling stiff and abused from yesterday's fall down the well and then from having Caroline Webster land on top of her today. She hadn't felt this battered since she'd run track and field in high school. Heather figured that she had a half hour until six, which was when dinner had been served last night. When she got back to her room she undressed, put on her robe and padded down the hall to the bathroom.

The huge bathroom had a claw foot tub that Heather filled three quarters of the way up with water as hot as she could stand. Slowly she submerged herself in the tub, which was long enough for her to comfortably stretch out. Muscle by tired muscle the heat slowly loosened and drained away the tension of the last two days. She wiggled her legs in front of her and leaned back to release the tightness in her back. Then she just lay there, completely relaxed, and stared up at the paint flaking from the ceiling over twelve feet away.

So much needs to be done here, she thought dreamily, but what a pleasure it would be to do it all. Her eyes closed. A sharp knock came at the bathroom door.

"Yes?" Heather called out.

"I just brought your tray up, Miss," Mrs. Maxwell asked through the door. "Shall I leave it in your room or would you like me to bring it back to the kitchen to keep it warm?"

"Leave it in my room, Mrs. Maxwell. I'm almost done here. By the way," she called out, "Do you know when Mr. Compton will be getting back?"

"All I know is that he's at a dinner meeting and he'll be back later."

Probably a meeting with Ms. Gorgeous Body, Heather thought bitterly. Some meeting! Giving herself a vigorous toweling and slipping into a sweatshirt and jeans, Heather went down the hall to her room. The small table next to her bed had been cleared for the tray, and the one straight-backed chair had been placed in front of the table. A rather stark look, it gave her the feeling that she had been sent to her room for being naughty.

Well, at least the condemned woman will eat a hearty meal, Heather thought as she looked over the breast of chicken with corn bread, sweet potatoes and green beans that filled her plate. For a moment she wondered if she was too tired to eat, but after a few bites, her appetite returned and she cleaned the plate. Finding some macaroons on another plate covered with a napkin next to a pot of tea, Heather sat back and savored their sweetness, thinking that Mrs. Maxwell really was a treasure. She might not be much for conversation, but her meals sure spoke volumes.

After finishing her second cup of tea, Heather sat in the chair for a moment and wondered what to do next. Is this why the rich always look so bored? she wondered. When you don't have to cook and clean up after yourself, is there just too much free time? Heather knew this wasn't really the problem for her. She was a guest whose visit was over; this was just the long down time until saying a final farewell. Caroline didn't strike her as the forgiving kind, and she'd probably prefer to think that Heather was responsible for the accident than believe that an attempt had been made on her life.

"I may as well make the most of my remaining time here," Heather said out loud to the empty room. "What is there that I would really like to do in this house that will only take an hour or so?"

The idea of finding the portrait of the three Compton brothers that her mother had done immediately came to mind. Jack had told her that the paintings had been stored in the attic. Maybe a short search would give her a chance to see a piece of her mother's early work, something she had done before Heather was born. Smiling at the thought of being able to tell her mother that she had seen the painting, Heather changed out of her sweat clothes and into her jeans and a sweater. Then she went down the hall opening doors, trying to find access to the attic.

Just past the main stairwell she opened a door which revealed nothing but darkness. Heather felt around for a light switch. When she pushed the button, the dim bulb illuminated a long flight of dusty wooden stairs. Carefully she made her way up the steep steps. When she reached the top, there was no light switch available, but fortunately there were full windows that let in the light of the fading day. The attic was divided up into a number of rooms off of a main hallway. Of course, Heather thought, this would have been quarters for the servants in the last century during the house's heyday when a large staff would have been needed to keep it running.

Heather walked down the hall to the end where there was a second stairway, which she guessed would probably lead down to the kitchen. The servants' stairs, so they could get to their rooms without going through the house. Heather made her way back along the hall, inspecting each room. All the doors were open, except for the last room she came to. That door was either locked or jammed. Taking the skeleton key that Michael had given her out of her pocket, she shoved it into the lock and turned. The bolt stiffly released from the latch, and Heather pushed the door open.

There was a metal bed frame along one wall with a simple wooden chair next to it. Along the other wall, carelessly stacked and partially covered with an old bed sheet, were several large paintings. There was just enough light coming through the windows that she could make out the general subject of each painting. She studied each one, then carefully placed it to one side against the bed frame. Toward the end, Heather came across a painting that seemed to fit the description of the one her mother had painted: three men by a fireplace. Two were seated in chairs in a conversational position and the third was standing further back, as if he had only accidentally stepped into the picture.

Although the painting was heavy in its ornate frame, Heather carried it to the stairwell and propped it up on the steps where the yellow electric light gave her a chance to examine it. The man sitting on the right was probably Leo, she thought, because he appeared to be in his fifties. That meant the other seated figure was Michael's father, Anthony. He was thin and smiling, and definitely the only one who appeared to be enjoying the experience. Standing behind the others with his face turned so that it was half in darkness stood Alex. Although her mother had been rather impressionistic in portraying his features, there was a dark, brooding quality to the face that made him the focus of the painting. The other two men might be easily overlooked, but Alex jumped from the canvas and seized the viewer's attention.

Heather smiled to herself. As with so much of her mother's work, she was at her best when vividly portraying those people for whom her feelings were, at best, ambivalent. Her paintings of friends and family were competent, but not inspired. But give her an unscrupulous computer whiz, an oil baron, or a thrice-divorced socialite, and her mother's work transcended the ordinary. Alex Compton had clearly served as an inspiration to her, even if she considered him to be somehow evil.

Not able to help herself, Heather found she was staring at his face, wishing irrationally that the firelight in the picture had been brighter so she could make out his features more clearly. There was something about him that was decidedly intriguing. She felt as if she knew the man well enough to imagine what he might say next or how he would hold his head when making a reply.

Well, Mom, you've done it again, she thought to herself as she carried the painting upstairs and replaced it in front of the others. She carefully put them back against the wall, placing her mother's on the outside, covered them all again with the sheet, then locked the door. No need to let others know she'd been spying, Heather thought, as she went back to the main hall. About to go down the stairs, she thought she heard a noise from the direction of the servants' stairs. Heather paused for a moment. Should she see what had made the sound? When it didn't happen again, she decided to leave well enough alone. No need to get caught prowling around in the attic.

Heather had just returned to her room when there was a knock on the door. When she pulled it open, Michael was standing in the doorway.

"Oh, it's you," she said coolly. "We need to talk."

"Sure, we can talk later. Right now we're having a meeting downstairs, and we'd like you to be there."

"No. We need to talk now. I met Renata Sisco this

afternoon. You do remember her, don't you? Your fiancée."

"Renata was *here*!"

"Yes. I can see how you might be surprised. I'm sure it wasn't part of your plan to have your fiancée meet . . ." Heather almost said 'your girlfriend,' but decided that was giving their relationship too much standing, "someone you're dating."

Michael reached out and grabbed her by the arms before she could back away.

"Look, I know this looks bad, and we don't have time to talk right now," he said gruffly. "But you have to trust me, I can explain everything."

"Come along, you two," Caroline said, hobbling past the doorway on a cane. "Time for chitchat later."

Michael and Heather followed her downstairs without speaking.

## Chapter Ten

George Webster and Thornton Jennings were seated across from each other in front of the fireplace. For a fleeting moment, Heather wondered if they were sitting in the same chairs that Anthony and Leo had been in when her mother had painted them. The fireplace certainly looked to be the one in the picture.

"Hello, Heather," George Webster said warmly, taking her hand. He introduced her to the lawyer, who gave her a polite smile.

Heather sat next to Michael on the love seat, pushing herself as far away from him as possible, and Caroline sat on a large stuffed chair that had apparently been moved into the parlor since last night. Her injured ankle had been wrapped in an elastic bandage and was propped up on a hassock.

"We're having this meeting," George said, looking at Heather, "because of the number of strange occurrences that have taken place at the house in the last few days. Since you've been present when several of them have taken place, we thought that having your input would be valuable."

Heather nodded cautiously.

"For the sake of accuracy let me enumerate the incidents that have occurred. Two days after we indicated at the official probate of Uncle Leo's will that we intended to move into the house, we received an anonymous threatening letter at our apartment in Boston warning us against coming to live in the Compton House. Two others followed. On our first night in residence, a week later, a mirror was broken and the furniture in our bedroom was splattered with pig's blood. Then there was the destruction of our mailbox shortly after that, followed by the attack on Anna the night before last. Then there was the rather mysterious fragment of a conversation that Heather heard through the open window."

He repeated it for the group.

Caroline frowned. "You never told me about that," she said to her husband, while managing to capture Heather in her accusing glare.

"I didn't see any point in alarming you since you appeared determined to stay here. And, at any rate, the conversation didn't clearly relate to our problems."

"Heather did fall down the well right afterwards," Michael said.

"But we have agreed that was an accident, haven't we?" George countered calmly.

Heather debated whether to tell them about the face she thought she saw over the edge of the well and the can of paint that had mysteriously disappeared from the dining room. Finally, she decided to keep quiet. The first could be dismissed as imaginary and the second could be considered a mistake on her part, and she didn't want to expose herself to any more of Caroline's criticism.

"This was followed by 'Get Out' being written on the dining room wall yesterday afternoon," George went on. "And today Michael reported to me that we had an intruder in the house last night."

"Which you never told me about," Caroline said to Heather.

"I told Heather that I would tell you about it, so she left it up to me," said Michael. "I had to leave before you were out of bed this morning, but I did call George and report it to him. So if there's anyone to blame, it should be me."

"And finally," George continued patiently, "there was the ladder incident of this afternoon in which Caroline was injured."

Caroline wiggled her ankle as if to prove the fact.

"Apparently, Lloyd believes that the step on the ladder had been tampered with, is that right?" George said to Heather.

"Yes. He thinks it was cut with a saw."

George nodded and turned to Thornton Jennings, who had been sitting quietly but attentively throughout.

"As you can see, Thornton, there has been a concerted effort by someone to see that we don't inherit this house."

"And whom do you suspect?" the lawyer asked.

"It has to be somebody in the town who still has a grudge against the Compton family," Caroline burst out. "Who else could it be?"

"Do you or the state police have any specific suspects?" Jennings asked.

"No," said Michael. "According to rumors there are a few people around town who still grumble about the things the Comptons did at one time or another. But the police have no solid leads."

"Is it true that if no member of the family stays in the house long enough to inherit, the house will be sold and the money will go to charity?" asked Heather.

The lawyer nodded. "That's basically correct."

"So these charities would gain if the Comptons could be scared out of the house."

"Yes," said Jennings with a smile. "I see where you're going, but I doubt that The American Cancer Society or The American Kidney Foundation would resort to such harassment."

Heather frowned. "I thought that maybe they were small local charities."

"No. Leo named only large national charities."

"Then you don't think that it's some troublemaker with a grievance against the Comptons doing this?" George asked Heather.

"I suppose it could be," Heather answered, "but whoever it is seems awfully persistent for someone nursing an old grudge."

"What about that business we asked you to check into, Thornton, about whether we have to spend the night in the house to meet the terms of the will?" Caroline asked, turning in her chair to face him and wincing with pain.

"I'm afraid the will is quite clear on that point. In order to inherit, a family member must live on the grounds of the estate, and that is specifically defined as spending at least six hours here between the hours six P.M. and six A.M."

"Uncle Leo must have been crazy," Caroline said with disgust.

"Well, it is a somewhat unusual requirement," Jennings said, "and we could go to court to try to break the

116    *Glen Ebisch*

will. But it would take a great deal of time and money, and if we lost, and you hadn't been living in the house, you'd have surrendered your opportunity to inherit."

"So what you're saying is that whether we go to court or not, we have to live in the house for three months," Michael said.

The lawyer nodded.

"What does 'on the grounds of the estate' mean exactly?" Heather asked.

The lawyer paused. "I suppose it would include the main house, the stables, and any other outbuildings."

"That's a big help," said Caroline. "I'm not about to live in the stables with Jack, and I certainly wouldn't be any safer there."

"I was just wondering," said Heather, "whether a vehicle parked on the grounds would qualify."

"You mean like a trailer or a camper?" asked Michael.

Thornton Jennings looked at Heather with a new appreciation. "I'll have to check. I don't believe a specific mention is made of residing in a permanent structure or dwelling, so that might be a possibility."

"You mean I could park a trailer out in front and live there instead of in this spooky old house," said Caroline, suddenly excited.

"Very possibly," said Jennings.

George Webster cleared his throat and turned to his wife. "Are you sure that would be any better? Would you really be any safer in a trailer?"

"A nice, small, brightly lit trailer would make a world of difference. We could get a doublewide so Michael could stay there, too. Then I'd feel safe. I could spend the required time every night in the trailer, then go anywhere I wanted."

"But, Caroline, would that really work in the long run?

Even if you last out the three months and get the house, there's no guarantee that this harassment will stop. Do you really want to live here in constant fear of your neighbors?" asked her husband.

"You simply don't want me to live here at all, George. Just admit it. You want me to move back to Boston and forget the whole thing." Caroline burst out, struggling to her feet and ignoring her husband's offer of assistance. "Well, I'm not going to forget it. This is the Compton House and I'm a Compton." She turned and walked out of the room, carrying her cane more than using it.

There was a moment of embarrassed silence.

"I'm afraid that Caroline isn't completely rational when it comes to this house," George finally said. "Her therapist thinks that in some way it's serving as an emotional replacement for her parents. She never adjusted normally to their deaths. I keep hoping that she'll have a breakthrough and change her mind about this folly, but it hasn't happened yet. If only she could spend a bit more time in Boston."

"Who's keeping track of whether Caroline and Michael are really spending the required amount of time here?" asked Heather.

George looked at her in surprise. "Nobody told you? That's the job of the executor of Leo's will."

"Who's that?" asked Heather.

"You've met him. It's Lloyd, Lloyd the gardener."

The manager of the estate, Heather thought, smiling to herself. Lloyd was quite the old fox.

George asked if anyone wanted sherry. Thornton Jennings accepted. Since it was clear that the two men wanted to discuss other business dealings, Heather and Michael walked out into the hall.

"Is there another room with furniture in it where we can sit?" she asked.

"Beats me, I've only lived here a couple of days myself. We could go up to my room."

Heather shook her head and grabbed a straight-backed chair from the hallway. "Let's go into the dining room."

Carrying a chair of his own, Michael followed her. Heather pushed the switch that turned on the large crystal chandelier in the center of the room. Empty of furniture and in semi-darkness, the room seemed cavernous, like a ballroom after the dancers had gone home.

"So why didn't you tell me you were engaged?" Heather asked, as soon they were seated in chairs facing each other.

"I'm not," Michael said.

Heather gave a disbelieving laugh. "You mean this Renata woman goes around lying about being engaged to you? Only a crazy person would do that, and she didn't look crazy to me."

"She's not crazy, at least not completely, just ambitious." Heather started to speak, but Michael held up his hand. "Let me explain this whole mess, then you can ask me any questions you want. Okay?"

Heather nodded.

"I met Renata about six months ago at a gallery in Boston that was showing the work of some contemporary younger artists. A small sculpture of hers was in the show. I've always been interested in finding new artists, so we started to talk about her work."

Seeing the skeptical look on Heather's face, he paused.

"Okay, I'll admit it, I might not have talked to her as long if she weren't attractive, but we did begin by discussing art. Eventually we started dating. It went fine at first. She acted very sweet, and was very interested in my work at the museum. We used to go to parties that other people involved with the museum gave, and people began to expect to see us together."

"You sound like a perfect couple," Heather said. She'd meant for it to sound sarcastic, but instead it came out as an honest opinion.

Michael nodded. "But then I started to hear stories. Friends would come to me looking kind of embarrassed and tell me how Renata had approached them about putting a piece of her work in their gallery or in an exhibition. She even suggested to some people that I would do them favors if they showed her works or, worse yet, shut them out of the museum shows, if they didn't help her."

"So she was using her relationship with you to promote her work," said Heather.

"Exactly. This all came to a head three months ago when she walked into my supervisor's office and said that she was my fiancée. She then had the nerve to suggest that her art be represented in a small experimental gallery that we were starting to set up to display contemporary works by Boston artists."

"But you said yourself that her work is good."

"That's the thing. Her work might have gotten in on its own merits, but she purposely lied and claimed to be my fiancée. My boss was furious, because she felt that I should have raised the matter with her myself. She didn't like having the artist come in and pressure her."

"Did you tell her that Renata wasn't your fiancée?"

"Of course. But that just made me look like someone who was dating a lunatic or someone who lied about whether he was engaged."

"What about Renata? I'm sure you brought all of this up with her."

"You bet I did. I first talked to her about it when she began approaching my friends. She said that if I really loved her I'd want her to succeed, and that since we were a couple, there was nothing wrong with her trading off of my position. I asked her not to do it any more, and reluctantly, she promised that she wouldn't. When I came to her after the museum episode, she said that we'd been going out for almost three months, so why not say she was my fiancée."

"What did you do?"

"I told her we were finished. That I wasn't going to see her again."

"That must have been hard. She's a very attractive woman."

"Not when you get to know her." Michael paused and a slight smile passed over his lips. "The hard thing is that she can make the most outrageous behavior some-how seem perfectly reasonable. She always made me feel guilty, like I was the one in the wrong. That I was being irrational."

"But if you broke up with her, why is her work being exhibited in the gallery?"

"When my supervisor got over being mad at me, she looked at some pictures that Renata had left and really liked her work. She decided to put her in the exhibition. I asked my boss not to, but she said that it was my own fault that I'd gotten into such an uncomfortable situation, and that was no reason to deny the public access to a fine young female sculptor."

"Is that why you decided to go on leave?"

Michael nodded. "I figured that if my boss was going to treat me that way, perhaps it was time to see if I could use my experience to find a new opportunity. And once I thought about it, I realized that maybe I'd gotten a bit stale after so many years working in the same place."

"Then why are you helping to set up Renata's exhibit?"

"That little experimental gallery is the only original idea of mine that I've managed to get my supervisor to support. She said that unless I helped get it organized, she'd cancel the whole thing. There are ten artists other than Renata being shown there; I felt that I owed it to them to bite the bullet and see Renata one last time."

"I understand," Heather said slowly, trying to digest it all.

Michael sighed. "You probably think I'm a fool to get involved with someone who would use me like that."

Heather thought back to all the times she'd given Richard money for paint or canvases. How his idea of a date was going out for fast food, then visiting some of his friends who were having an impromptu party at one of their studios. When she went back over all of her conversations with Richard, the lion's share of the time had been spent analyzing his hopes, dreams, and ambitions; her future had only been discussed when Richard was in a bad mood and became critical of her desire to excel as a decorative painter.

"It's easy to make a mistake like that," Heather said. "Better to be the one who was used than the one who did the using. But why was Renata out here today pretending to be your fiancée?"

"Yesterday at the museum she asked me where I'd been keeping myself, and I made the mistake of telling her a bit about where I was staying and why. Probably the idea of living in a mansion appealed to her, so she thought she'd come out and see for herself, still keeping up the pretense that we're engaged."

"Did you give her any reason to think that you'd come back to her?" Heather asked sharply.

"None at all. She apologized yesterday and suggested that we get back together, but I refused. Now that I see her for what she is, it's hard to imagine that I ever thought she loved me for myself. But she's persistent, and like most manipulative people, she thinks that her charm will win out over any obstacle."

An image flashed through her mind of Richard with his injured boyish smile telling her good-bye and how sorry he was to go but his opportunities were in New York. Her anger had been incomprehensible to him because it never entered Richard's narrow understanding that anyone would ever be upset with him for doing what was in his own interest. He was the sun, so why should the planets resent traveling around him?

"And what about today? Mrs. Maxwell said you were in Boston again."

"No, I was . . . somewhere else. I'd rather not tell you about it just yet, but I promise you it had nothing to do with Renata. I'm done with her." Michael stood up and went the two steps it took to reach Heather. She stood up as well and for a moment they faced each other without speaking.

"Do you believe me?" he asked.

She nodded.

"Are you willing to give us a try?"

Heather stepped forward until her body was pressing against Michael's. She turned her face up to his and felt his lips meet hers. Michael's arm came behind her back and held her close as they shared a lingering kiss.

"Is that a 'yes'?" he asked in a thick voice a few moments later when they stepped apart.

"That's not the way I say good-bye," Heather replied.

She wanted nothing more than to kiss him again. To spend the evening in his arms and forget that there was anything else in the world that they needed to worry about. But she knew that wasn't true.

"What are we going to do about this house, Michael? Things are getting out of hand."

Michael sighed and ran a hand over his forehead. "George is right. Caroline is obsessed with this place. It isn't healthy. Whatever she lost when Mom and Dad died isn't going to be restored by returning the Compton House to its earlier glory."

"Why does she feel that way? What happened when your parents died that threw her for a loop?"

"I was away at college when my dad had his first heart attack. They were living in Maine near Portland, and Caroline was working for Dad, handling the paperwork for the lumber yard. After he had heart surgery, Dad decided to sell the business, which had been losing money for several years, and invest what he got for it in a retirement fund. Before Dad could sell out, my mother had a serious stroke. Dad sold the business for a lot less than it was worth and put Mom in the best nursing home he could find."

"How sad," said Heather. "What happened to Caroline?"

"Well, she lost her job when Dad sold the business. At first she was going to get another job to help out, but Dad was pretty frail and what with visiting Mom twice a day every day, he really need someone at home to take care of him."

"How long did that go on?"

"For almost three years. It ended in the spring of my senior year. Dad and Caroline would bring Mom home for the occasional holiday. She recognized family members, but it was pretty hard to tell how much she was aware of her surroundings. But Dad thought she seemed to know when she was home, and he liked having her there for special occasions. So they brought her home for Easter that year. She came home on Saturday and was going to stay overnight until Sunday. I had a big senior project I was working on and couldn't get away."

Michael paused and stared hard across the dimly lit dining room as if reliving the events of that weekend.

"What happened?" Heather gently prodded.

"No one is exactly sure. Mom tended to get confused when she was away from the home overnight. She was in the bedroom next to Dad's; she seemed to get more restless when they shared a bed. Sometime in the night she got up. Usually she needed a wheelchair, but that night she somehow managed to get to the kitchen on her own. She must have brought some matches back to her room and lit a decorative candle that was on her dresser. The fire investigator figured that it fell or somehow got too near the drapes and they caught on fire. When the firemen got there that entire part of the house where my father and mother were sleeping was engulfed in flames."

"What happened to Caroline?"

"She was on the other side of the house in the guest room. By the time she smelled smoke and called the fire department it was too late. She tried to get to their rooms. She was still in the house trying to get to them when the firemen arrived. They had to drag her out. She had some pretty bad second-degree burns and was suffering from smoke inhalation."

"And, of course, Caroline blamed herself," said Heather.

Michael nodded. "I tried to tell her that it was one of those tragedies where nobody was to blame. But she blamed herself for letting Mom stay overnight, for not removing the candle from her room, for not waking up when Mom was wandering around, and for not smelling smoke sooner and rescuing them."

"You can tell somebody not to feel guilty, but it doesn't help."

"Just makes it worse," said Michael. "Every excuse I made for her seemed to motivate her to find another way to beat herself up. Finally I just stopped talking about it with her. I suggested that maybe she should get counseling, but she wouldn't do it. I think she felt that was a way of weaseling out of just punishment for what she'd done."

"But finally she met George Webster."

"She moved to Boston after a couple of years and got a job in a large accounting firm. That's what she had trained for at school. Her firm handled the books for George's company. That's how they met. And somehow under all the brittleness and self-loathing, he managed to see the kind and loving woman she had been before the disaster. They've been married almost five years now. But I'm sure it hasn't always been easy for him, and dealing with this house has only made things more difficult."

"George mentioned something about counseling."

"George managed to get her to seek help, and I think she's made a lot of progress. But you can see it being undone more and more every day she spends in this house. Caroline seems to feel that all the bad things that are happening here are little tests to see if this time she'll come through and save the family. She failed once before, and this time she's determined not to. But it's destroying her."

"What would you like me to do?" Heather asked. She had entered the room determined to leave the house as soon as possible; but now that she had forgiven Michael and come to a greater understanding of why Caroline was so difficult, it seemed that she should make some offer of assistance.

"Would you stay tonight?" Michael asked in an almost pleading tone. "I don't know what's going to come of all this talk about trailers. Maybe by morning, George will have talked some sense into her, and she'll go back home to Boston."

"Of course I'll stay." Heather stood up and looked around the room. The blue walls had taken on a blue-black color in the dim light, something like the sky just after sunset. "I think Caroline should leave. This place is unhealthy for her. My only regret is that if no one inherits, the house will be destroyed."

Michael looked at her and smiled. "The place has really gotten to you, hasn't it?"

Heather nodded.

"You're more of a Compton than I am."

"I hope not," Heather said. "I'd hate to find out that we're related. That would be just too gothic for words."

"Well, I don't want to raise your hopes, but don't give up on the house just yet," said Michael. He put his arm around her and guided her out into the hallway.

"What does that mean?" Heather asked, trying to read the expression on his face.

"Right now it means that tomorrow is another day; and whatever will be will be."

"Wow! Two platitudes from the movies in one sentence. You're my kind of guy."

Michael tightened his arm around her as they went up the sweeping staircase. "Let me keep lookin' at you, kid, and you'll never go hungry again."

## Chapter Eleven

Heather thought she had been asleep for hours when she heard the sound. It took a minute for her to register that the annoying buzz was coming from her cell phone which was on the floor beside her bed. Turning on the lamp, she glanced at the clock, which read one A.M. Not that late at all.

"Hello," she mumbled.

"Hi. Just thought I'd check in before you went to bed," said Abby.

"You're too late."

"Oops! I just got back from my date," Abby said, ending on an upnote that told Heather she wanted to be asked about it.

"How was your date?" she dutifully asked.

"Jim is a really great guy. His dad was a painter, and Jim used to work with him when he was a kid."

"Guess that gave you a lot in common to talk about," said Heather, struggling to keep her eyes open.

"You better believe it. He knows almost as much about faux painting techniques as I do."

"That's nice."

"He's going to college part time to get his degree in finance."

"Good."

"And he has a great tattoo of Elvis on his rear end."

Heather was about to mumble her reply, when her eyes shot open. "What did you say?"

"Just checking to see if you were paying attention."

"Very funny," Heather said, now fully awake. "Well, I've got some news for you."

She then told Abby about the ladder breaking and about the family meeting. Finally she filled Abby in on Michael's explanation concerning Renata Sisco.

"So, do you believe him?" Abby asked.

"Yes, I do," Heather said with so much firmness that she surprised herself. "I guess you had to be here to see the expression on his face and hear his tone of voice."

"I guess I'd believe him, too," said Abby. "Guys usually won't admit to being made to look stupid by a woman unless they're telling the truth. This Renata must be quite a character."

"Sort of the female equivalent of Richard," said Heather.

Abby chuckled. "Now that you mention it, there are similarities. Do you think this woman is going to give up that easily?"

"Michael thinks it's all over with, but I'm not so sure. She sounds like someone who could be pretty determined, if she figures there's a mansion to be gained as part of the deal."

"Doesn't sound like that particular mansion is much of a bargain. Do you think that Caroline Webster is going to stay there camped out in her double-wide?"

"It's hard to say. She's hanging on by a thread right now."

"So are my eyelids, and I've got to be back at the Burger Hut by eight and paint three more hamburger people on the walls. Do you know how hard it is to make a hamburger roll look human?"

"When do you think you'll be finished?"

"If all goes well, I should be out of there by noon. What are you up to tomorrow?"

"Hard to say. I guess if Caroline stays around, I'll be stenciling the dining room."

"Okay. I'll be there by the early afternoon to give you a hand. I'm kind of looking forward to seeing the house of horrors up close again."

"Be careful what you wish for," Heather warned.

After Heather turned off the phone, she rolled over on her side toward the window, hoping that it wouldn't take her long to go back to sleep. The room had been stuffy when she had gone to bed, so she had opened the window about an inch. Now there was a chilly breeze coming in right on her face. Heather tried pulling the blanket higher, almost covering her head. That seemed to help, but just as she was starting to doze off again something else intruded on the edge of her consciousness. The smell of leaves burning. Heather smiled to herself at the thought of a lovely fall day and the crackle of the leaves with their edges curling up in a pungent fire.

She sat up in bed! This wasn't a fall day. It was a night in spring. She rushed to the window that looked out on the front of the house. Off to the left, by the corner of the house, a fire was burning right under a pine that was silhouetted by moonlight against the night sky. As she watched, a flame leapt up from the fire and caught one of the lower branches. Happy to have found fuel, the flames danced from branch to branch and in seconds the entire tree was burning like a fifty-foot torch.

Heather rushed out of her room and down the hall to Michael's. She banged on the door.

"Who is it?" he finally called after what seemed to Heather like an hour.

"It's Heather. There's a fire in front of the house."

"A what?"

A few seconds later the door flew open. Struggling into his bathrobe as he ran, Michael went down the hall to the master suite. When George finally answered his knock, Michael spoke to him in a soft voice, then returned to Heather's side.

"George is going to call the emergency number. They have a volunteer fire department in Compton, so I don't know how long it will take them to get here."

"Is there anything we can do in the meantime?" she asked.

"Yes. Get dressed and meet me out front."

Heather pulled her jeans and sweatshirt over her T-shirt and gym shorts. By the time she reached the front door, Michael was there.

"I saw a hose at that end of the house the other day. I guess Lloyd uses it to water the garden. At least we can hose down the side of the house."

As they got nearer to the burning tree, Heather could see that it was a good seventy-five feet from the house, a bit further than she had imagined, but still close enough that embers were floating over onto the roof. Fortunately, there wasn't more wind, she thought, or this could be a real problem. The heat from the tree toasted her face as she helped Michael unroll the hose. The smell of burning pine caught in her throat and made her gag.

"I noticed that tree was dead when I first arrived. I wonder why Lloyd didn't have it taken down," Michael said.

Michael walked back from the house, while Heather turned on the water. A thin stream came shooting up to hit right at the middle of the second floor.

"There's not enough water pressure to reach the roof," Michael shouted as a flurry of embers caught a breeze and floated onto the top of the house.

Heather looked up at the roof.

"We might reach it from that garret window in the attic," she said.

"How would we get the hose up there?"

"I have a ball of twine in the van. If we tied one end around the hose and the other around something heavy, could you throw it up to that window?"

"I suppose," said Michael, judging the distance.

"Well, I could catch it and haul up the front of the house. Then I'd be able to reach those embers."

"It's worth a try."

Heather ran to the van and got the twine. It was a fifty-foot ball. That should be enough, she thought. Now for something to tie it to. It couldn't be too heavy, and it had to be balanced enough that it could be thrown with some accuracy. As Heather rooted around in the back of the van, George and Caroline came out of the house. George was almost dragging Caroline, who kept turning back as if to return inside. She was wearing only her nightgown.

"Where are the fire trucks?" she asked Heather. "Where are the fire trucks?"

George held her closer. "They're coming, dear."

"Not again. Oh no, no, not again," she cried, staring up at the blazing tree, then pressing her face into his chest.

"Have you found something to throw?" Michael asked, running up to the van.

Caroline grabbed his shirt front. "You've got to save the house, Michael. You weren't there the last time. This time you've got to do something."

"I will," Michael said, brushing her hair back from her face and managing to give her a smile. "I don't think she should be here, George."

George nodded. "We'll go to the stable. We'll send Jack around to help you."

"Where's Mrs. Maxwell?" Heather asked, suddenly remembering the cook.

"We met her in the hall as we were leaving." said George. "She was going to leave by the kitchen door and go to the stable until it was safe."

Caroline gave a low moan.

"She's shaking," George said, holding her more tightly.

Heather reached in the back of the van and pulled out an old flannel shirt that she used on the job. It was splattered with paint, but would help keep the woman warm. As she pulled it out, a plastic pint water bottle fell onto the ground.

"That should do it," said Michael, picking it up eagerly. "If I fill this with water, we can tie the twine around it, then I can throw it sort of like a football. I'll go fill it up."

"I'll go upstairs and get ready to catch it," said Heather.

She turned to run back into the house, but Michael suddenly grabbed her arm.

"Are you sure you want to do this?" he asked softly. "We can always wait for Jack. I don't like the idea of you going back inside the house."

"There's no time. If it looks like the house is going to catch fire, I'll be out in a flash," Heather said. "I'll go upstairs to the attic and open the right window. You be warming up your passing arm."

Michael held onto her for a moment, then he nodded.

Heather raced back into the house. Even though there was little chance of its burning down, there was something counterintuitive about going back inside. She pushed those fears out of her mind as she darted up the stairs to the second floor. By the time she reached the top of the attic stairs, her breath was coming hard and her heart was pumping.

The scant illumination from the light over the stairwell was just enough that she could find her way to the window in the room right across from the stairs. Having gotten her bearings by looking out, she rushed down the hall to the attic room nearest the burning tree. When she got to the end of the hall, she realized with surprise that it was the room that held the paintings.

She reached in the pocket of her jeans and was relieved to find that the skeleton key was still there. She quickly opened the door. Carefully walking around the stacked pictures, she tried to open the window. It was stuck. Warped from the dampness or painted shut, she thought. From the back pocket of her jeans she pulled out her pocketknife. Wedging the thickest blade between the sill and window frame, she began forcing the window open. The sound of the splintering wood was painful to hear, but this was no time to be worrying about finish carpentry. Finally the seal broke, and the window reluctantly rose.

"Okay, Michael," she shouted.

"Stand back from the window," he called. "I'm not sure how accurate I'll be. I might hit the glass."

His first throw was short and bounced on the roof out of Heather's reach. The second was too far off to the left side.

"Guess I'm a little rusty," Michael called, sounding almost like he was enjoying himself.

His third throw was right on target, but fell a couple of feet short. Fortunately a protruding wooden roof shingle stopped the bottle before it could roll off the roof. Heather quickly reached out and snagged the twine.

"Got it!" she called, pulling on the twine and hauling the hose up the front of the house. "Turn it on!" she said, when she had the nozzle in her hand.

Miraculously the old wooden roof shingles hadn't caught fire, but the wooden gutters, packed with years of dry debris, were filled with small blazes. She hosed those down, then carefully trained the water on every ember that floated onto the roof.

As quickly as it had begun, the fire stopped. With the tree completely consumed and no other dead or dry brush around, the fire quickly went out just as the fire engines came up the road. Heather carefully lowered the hose back down the front of the house.

She was about to leave the room when she stopped. She'd heard that fires sometimes started up again. Wasn't it better to be safe than sorry? She took the sheet off the stack of painting and removed her mother's. She carried it downstairs and placed it in her room. At least I can rescue it on the run, if I have to, she told herself.

When she returned outside, some firemen were putting ladders up against the front of the house while others were hosing down the smoldering tree. Michael and Jack were standing together with one fireman who seemed to be in charge.

"Having a dead tree right next to the house like that is pretty dangerous," the fireman said to Michael.

Michael nodded. "I've just moved in here. Why didn't Lloyd have it taken down?" he asked Jack.

"I told Lloyd that I could do it, but he said it was too big a job and we needed a professional. I guess Uncle Leo didn't want to pay for one, so the tree stayed."

"Did anyone see how the fire started?" the fireman asked.

Heather stepped forward. "I didn't see the fire start, but there was a small fire already going under tree before it caught fire."

"Was there brush piled there?" the fireman asked Jack sharply.

"No," Jack said. "But there was a pile of leaves that we'd raked up on the side of the house. Lloyd and I were going to haul it away at the end of the week."

"Could some of it have blown under the tree?" asked Michael.

"Not enough wind," the fireman said. "And we still need to know where the spark came from."

"You make it sound like the fire might have been set," said Michael.

"There's always that possibility." He gave Michael a long look that indicated he knew something about the history of the Comptons. "Under the circumstances."

Too tired to discuss the matter further, Heather turned to go back inside the house.

"Where are you going, lady?" the fireman asked.

"To bed. Isn't the house safe?"

He paused for a moment. "Yeah, I guess it is. My men are just cleaning out the ash from the gutters. So I guess it's safe."

"Great. See you in the morning," she said and walked up to the front door.

Michael was beside her before she got the door open.

"You were wonderful tonight, Heather. I'm sure things would have been a lot worse if you hadn't come up with that hose idea."

He put his arms around her and gave her a hug. She weakly hugged him back.

"Thanks. And I'm sure I'll be proud of myself in the morning, but right now all I want is some sleep. If the fire starts up again, don't bother to wake me."

Michael smiled. "I'll come into your bedroom and carry you to safety personally."

Heather managed a faint grin. "Will you throw me over your back in the fireman's carry?"

"I was thinking of something a bit more romantic. Perhaps holding you in my arms, the way a husband carries his wife over the threshold."

"You'd never make it down the first flight of stairs."

"We'll try it some day. You'd be surprised."

"I bet I would."

## Chapter Twelve

A soft knock on her door brought Heather to full alertness. "I may as well sleep in my clothes in this place," she grumbled. But since the clock read seven-thirty, she realized that she had no grounds for complaint. She staggered to the door and pulled it open. Michael stood there dressed in a dark blue suit looking very handsome and professional.

"Are you planning to carry me downstairs dressed like that?" she asked.

"No need. The fire is definitely out, and there was only minimal damage," he said. "That's the good news."

"What's the bad news?"

"Caroline left last night. Seeing the fire was too much for her. It brought back all her guilt over Mom and Dad's deaths."

"Oh, no!"

Michael nodded. "She and George decided that staying here wasn't good for her. They're making an appointment with her therapist in Boston this morning, and she won't be returning."

"Poor Caroline. I hope being away from this place helps her."

"So do I."

"And I guess this means that the Compton house goes to charity," said Heather. "So my job here is done."

"Would you be willing to stay just for one more day?"

"Why?"

"Well," Michael hesitated. "I have a meeting I have to go to today, and I'd like you to be here tonight so I can talk to you about it."

"This is all pretty mysterious. Can't you tell me more than that?"

"I guess my few days in this place have made me kind of superstitious, but I'd rather not talk about this until it's a certainty. Can you wait until tonight?"

Heather nodded. "But what will I do here all day?"

"Why don't you keep on working in the dining room? You may as well. No matter what happens, I'm sure George will pay to see the job completed."

Stenciling walls that are going to be torn down isn't my idea of creative work, Heather thought. But she decided not to argue with Michael when things were going so badly for him.

"The only thing that worries me is that I don't like the idea of your being alone in the house," he went on.

"There's nothing to worry about. Now that Caroline is gone the vandalism will probably stop. I'll bet that everyone in Compton knows by now that she's left. No one cares about me. Anyway, Abby will be here by this afternoon to help me."

"Are you sure you don't mind staying?"

"Go do what you have to do and don't worry about me. I have a feeling that the worst of this is over."

Michael came toward her.

"Don't kiss me. I haven't brushed my teeth yet."

"And you smell like a fireplace," he added, taking her in his arms.

He pressed his lips to hers.

"You find peculiar things sexy," Heather said, when he'd released her, and she was back to breathing normally.

Michael looked at her, and Heather became aware that once again she was wearing only a T-shirt and shorts.

He smiled. "I don't think you look that peculiar."

Heather spent an extra long time in the bathroom getting the smell of smoke washed out of her hair and off of her body. Fortunately she had brought a second pair of jeans and a chambray work shirt, so she had something to change into. She didn't want to impose on Mrs. Maxwell to do her wash.

After her bath, she went directly to the kitchen. Mrs. Maxwell was working at the counter, and Jack was sitting at the table with a cup of coffee.

"How's the hero of Compton House this morning?" he asked with a grin.

"I wasn't much of a hero, and I'm a little worse for wear," Heather replied.

"You're in better shape than Caroline," said Jack. "She really lost it last night."

"I heard."

"You saw Michael before he left for his meeting this morning, then?" asked Jack, giving her a knowing smile.

Heather nodded, hating to admit that she had seen Michael in her bedroom at dawn. She could just imagine the gossip going all around the small town.

"I guess with Caroline's leaving that means the Compton House will be sold," said Jack.

"I suppose," said Heather. "What will you do when they close up the house?"

Jack shrugged. "I've saved up quite a bit. Maybe I'll go back to school full time. Or maybe I'll head out to Lenox and try getting a job as a waiter at one of those fancy restaurants."

"And what about you, Mrs. Maxwell? What will you do?" Heather asked.

Mrs. Maxwell looked up briefly from where she was carefully wiping the counter, but she kept her eyes focused on the floor as though a bit embarrassed at being asked.

"Oh, there are always jobs for women willing to cook."

"Did Uncle Leo leave you anything in his will to tide you over if the house was sold?" Heather asked.

Mrs. Maxwell caught Jack's eye for a moment.

"Leo Compton wasn't a guy who gave much away," Jack said with a loud laugh. "Not that he had much cash left by the time he died. We each got two months' salary as a token for our services."

"What about Lloyd?"

"I think he got a little more because he was put in charge of seeing that any relatives who got the house kept to the rules of the will," said Jack.

"I wonder if the house will sell quickly," Heather said.

Jack shrugged. "Don't know. Will you be leaving now that your job is finished?"

"Not just yet," Heather replied. "Michael wants me to

finish the dining room. I'm going to work on the stenciling today."

"Seems like a waste of money," Mrs. Maxwell sniffed, "to decorate a house that's probably going to be torn down anyway."

"All I know is what Michael asked me to do," said Heather. It bothered her a bit that what she said was the truth. Michael's request made no sense to her either, and yet he had asked her to wait until this evening for an explanation.

She headed for the door to the dining room.

"Could I have some coffee, juice, and toast whenever you get a chance?" she asked Mrs. Maxwell.

The woman nodded grimly, as if the waste of money still bothered her.

"See you later," Heather said to Jack.

Jack frowned. "Yeah. I know Lloyd's going to be on me about that fire. He'll claim that somehow that pile of leaves blew under that pine tree."

"But you said there was no way that could have happened."

"It would have to travel over a hundred feet. That won't matter to Lloyd," Jack said with a grim smile. "He'll still find some way to blame me."

Heather shook her head in sympathy and went down the side hall to the dining room. She stood in the middle of the room and tried to imagine which of the many stencil patterns would be appropriate. Maybe I can go wider than usual, she thought, as a kind of tribute to Caroline. Remembering that she still had a book of stencil patterns in her van that she had intended to show Caroline, Heather went out to the front of the house. Lloyd was standing there gazing at the burned pine.

"It doesn't look like much now, but it was quite a fire," Heather said, walking over to him.

Lloyd nodded. "Must have been. Jack said that you saw a fire on the ground right under the tree."

"Yes."

"Wasn't anything particular there when I left yesterday afternoon."

"Jack said there was some debris around the side of the house."

"Yep. But not out here. Only a fool would put a pile of dry leaves under a dead pine."

They stared in silence at the blackened tree as if it held some answers.

"I didn't know you were in charge of making sure that the heirs lived in the house for the right number of hours a day."

Lloyd nodded, and a hint of pride passed over his face. "Leo came up with that crazy scheme right after his last heart attack. He had me come up to his bedroom and told me how he wanted the house to go to a Compton, but only if they were going to live there. Otherwise he'd rather have the house and property sold and the money go to charity."

"How do you check on whether Caroline and Michael are staying here six hours a night?"

"I have my ways," he said, putting a finger beside his nose and giving her a wink.

"But what's the point of the will? Couldn't Leo see that requiring someone to live here for three months wouldn't guarantee that they would stay? Once a Compton owned the house, he or she could sell it."

"Sure. But he knew that only Caroline and Michael were left. I guess he wanted to test them to see if either one of them cared enough about the place to make an effort. Maybe he figured that sticking it out here wouldn't be real easy, but if one of them did, that person wouldn't want to sell the place and leave."

"Do you think some people from town are doing all this? That maybe one of them started the fire."

"At first I thought it might be some folks with hard feelings. That business with the pig's blood and the mailbox could have been done by folks with country ways. And somebody from town might have wanted to scare Anna. But I don't really see anyone waltzing in here and cutting your ladder or writing on the walls."

"What about setting the fire?"

Lloyd frowned. "That's taking things a bit far even for an old grudge."

"You know that Caroline Webster was pretty shocked by the whole thing because of what had happened to her parents."

"I heard she gave up and left."

"Did you know her parents had died in a fire?"

"Yep. Leo told me when it happened, must have been nine or ten years ago now."

"Did you spread it around town?" asked Heather.

Lloyd's face turned red. "I don't go talking out of school, missy. When Leo told me stuff about the family, it stayed between him and me."

"So as far as you know, no one else in town would have known."

He stared at her for a moment, puzzled. Then he smiled with comprehension.

"I see where you're going with this. Nobody in town would have known that Caroline Webster was especially afraid of fire."

"Right, so I'm just wondering if the fire was started

by someone who knew what had happened to her parents."

Lloyd held up three gnarled fingers. "That would be her brother, her husband, and me. Do you think I'm the most likely suspect, missy?" His tone sounded amused rather than afraid.

"It's crossed my mind," Heather admitted, smiling to take away any sting from the words. "But I don't see that you'd have anything to gain."

Lloyd chuckled. "You're right there. Leo gave me a few thousand in his will to make sure his little scheme went the way he wanted. I don't get any more no matter what happens to the house. Her husband, George, can't inherit. On the other hand, your friend Michael can go on living here now and get the house for himself if he wants."

"He doesn't care about the house," Heather said a bit more adamantly than she had intended.

"He told you that, did he?"

"Yes. Anyway, he doesn't want to spend the kind of money that it would take to fix this place up."

"Wouldn't have to," Lloyd said shortly. "Did he tell you about the man from the nursing home who came around a couple of days ago?"

Heather shook her head.

"Caroline told me about it. Guy came around who wants to put up a bunch of condominiums for old folks with a nursing home on the premises and everything. Offered her a couple of million for the house and land. She turned him down cold. Guess she told me about it because she wanted me to know that she had no intention of selling the house."

"Maybe Michael didn't know about it. Plus, he wouldn't cheat his sister in order to sell the house."

"I think you're right about that, missy. But he might do it for another reason." Lloyd looked off into the distance. "Could be for the best," said Lloyd. "You are more like Sarah Compton than Caroline will ever be."

"What's that supposed to mean?"

"You figure it out, missy."

Heather turned away from him and walked over to her van. She unlocked the door, took out her book of stencil samples, then slammed the door hard. At least slamming the door was one thing she *could* do. She couldn't deny what Lloyd had said, and she couldn't think of a good argument the other way. But at the same time she couldn't imagine Michael driving his own sister half-crazy for money. No matter how much. And he didn't seem to want the Compton House. Heck, I care for this place more than he does, she thought.

A chilling idea crossed her mind. Would Michael try to get this house for *me*? She pushed the thought away. All that rambling talk of Lloyd's about me and Sarah Compton, was that what he was getting at? That made no sense. The threats and vandalism had begun long before Michael and I met.

But what if . . . what if Michael had just been putting the finishing touch on someone else's pranks? She couldn't believe it. There was nothing sneaky or devious about him. She had to hold onto that thought. He wasn't Richard; he was the anti-Richard.

She carried the heavy book into the dining room and spent the next hour staring alternately at the pages in the book and at the upper part of the wall. Finally she settled on a pattern of small roses intertwined with leaves and stems. It was rather intricate but would look appropriate even if carried down quite low on the wall. She would do the roses in a deep carmine red and the stems in dark green. The leaves would be a light brown, much as they would look as they gently faded into autumn.

Heather smiled as she closed the book. This would be a challenging project. One that even Caroline, with her finicky taste, would appreciate, if she ever got to see it. Heather walked out to the van. She'd go and purchase the stencil and paints now, then take the opportunity to stop off at home to get more clothes. Even if she stayed only one more night, the smell of smoke made her one good shirt unwearable and she had to have something to put on after work. She could make the round trip and still be there in time for Abby right after lunch.

No one was in the kitchen, so she scribbled a note on the pad by the phone and left it on the table. No need to bother Mrs. Maxwell with preparing lunch.

Heather's first stop was at her paint supplies store, where she purchased the stencil and the necessary paint and brushes. As the bill mounted, Heather had a moment of concern. Passionate Painters wasn't doing so well that it could afford to lay out money without the certainty that the client would pay them back. She brushed her fears away. In the event that she wasn't able to complete the stenciling in the dining room, George Webster would probably be willing to compensate her for the materials. If not, she'd use them some time in the future on another job. One of the most disillusioning parts about being in business for yourself was running across the occasional person who refused to pay his bill, but she didn't think that would be a problem in this case.

When she reached home, Heather found that her mother had left a message asking her to call.

"How are things at the Compton House?" her mother immediately asked, skipping the formality of a 'hello'. Usually calm to the point of vagueness, this time her tone was sharp with concern. "I read in this morning's paper that there was a fire. I called your cell phone number but didn't get an answer."

Heather was surprised that a regional paper would have picked up the story. Perhaps one of the volunteer firefighters made a little extra money notifying the paper of local emergencies.

"I left the phone in the van while I was running some errands. Don't worry. I'm fine, and there was no damage to the house. A dead tree burned on the property." She purposely didn't mention how close the tree was to the house.

"Maybe it's too bad that the house didn't burn to the ground."

"Really, mother, it's not the house's fault. Anything strange going on out there is caused by people, not by ghosts."

"What strange things?"

I have to be more careful, Heather thought, she's really paying attention to what I'm saying, for a change.

"Oh, a mailbox was vandalized. That sort of thing."

The long pause on the other end told her that her mother knew she was being put off and would have liked more elaboration. Heather stubbornly refused to give it.

"Isn't your job out there done yet?" she asked.

"Probably in the next day or two. Abby will be out this afternoon to help me. That will make things go faster."

"Good. I'll feel better knowing that Abby is with you. She has a sensible head on her shoulders."

"Well, Michael Compton is there, too. He's sort of in charge now."

"What happened to his sister Caroline?"

"Caught me again," Heather muttered to herself.

"She decided to go back to Boston. The fire upset her. You know her parents died in a fire about ten years ago. By the way, how come you didn't mention that to me when I asked about the family?" she asked, trying to put her mother on the defensive.

"I believe that I was away working somewhere when it happened. But it does sound familiar. I must have gotten the story much later."

"Anthony and his wife both died."

"Poor Anthony. You know, I must have seen him a year or so before it happened. He was down in Boston to see someone, a heart specialist, I believe. I was walking on the street and by sheer coincidence we bumped into each other. He didn't look well, but his spirits were good. He showed me a photo of himself and his wife and children. He even had a wallet-sized picture of Alex, his wife, and his son Andrew. I believe they were living in Alaska."

"Did Alex still frighten you?" Heather explained that she had seen her mother's painting and how riveting Alex had appeared.

"I'm glad the painting is as effective as I remembered it," her mother said, with real pleasure in her voice. "But to answer your question, he looked rather sad. He had aged terribly. But it was more than just looking old, he also looked disappointed."

"How old would he have been?"

"Ten years ago he'd only have been in his early fifties. He had married a few years before to a woman a number of years younger according to Anthony. The boy must have been about nine or ten. He looked a great deal like his father."

"Alex and his son both died in a boating accident about seven years later."

"Oh, dear, now I feel rather guilty about the bad thoughts I've had about Alex for all this time. Perhaps the man wasn't actually evil at all, just cursed."

Heather smiled to herself and wondered, as she often did, whether some gypsy blood ran in her mother's family.

"Well, the painting is still a very good one. As you always say, a good work of art doesn't depend on what's actually there but on what the artist sees there."

"Yes. But like all artists I would like to believe that I see the truth beneath the appearances. I'd hate to think that all I painted were my fevered imaginings."

"I guess we'll never know for sure," said Heather. "When I get a chance to talk with Michael Compton again, I'll ask him if there was any family lore surrounding Alex after he left home. Maybe he'll turn out to be as evil as you thought."

"Yes, I suppose," her mother replied.

Heather could tell that her mother had gone off to a land of her own. In the art world Clarissa Martinson was known for her tendency to become so focused on her own thoughts that she was oblivious to what was right around her. When Heather was a child it had often been disconcerting to have her mother talking to her normally one second, then suddenly staring at a scene out the window as if no one else in the room existed. Heather had always been afraid to startle her when she went into these artistic trances. Like awakening a sleepwalker too suddenly, she was never sure what the effects would be.

"I'll give you a call once the job at the Compton House is over," she said softly.

"That will be fine, dear," her mother replied as if from a distance.

Before Heather could hang up the phone the line went

dead. Better to have her mulling over some aesthetic is-
sue than questioning me about my life, Heather concluded. The phone rang again. Uh, oh, maybe I relaxed
too soon.

"Hey, Heather," Abby shouted into the mouthpiece.
"Can you hear me?"

Over the background noise of machinery and people
talking, Heather could barely make out what Abby was
saying.

"Just about. What's going on?"

"I'm still at the Burger Hut. This place is a zoo at
lunch time. Look, I've got a problem. The regional manager showed up this morning, and he told Jim that the
humanoid hamburgers looked great, but he also wants
me to add French fries and a shake."

Heather hesitated, perplexed. "You mean he wants you
to paint fries and shakes that look sort of human?"

"You got it. We decided that the fries should be in
bags; otherwise they'd look too much like cartoon cig-
arettes, and that's the wrong image for the place."

"I see."

"But the shakes are tricky. I've been sketching cyl-
inders with eyes, but something's missing."

Heather thought for a moment. "Have the shake come
up above the rim of the cup in a kind of swirl, then make
the swirl look like stylized hair."

"Hang on, let me try it."

A full minute passed while Heather listened to the
background shouts of hungry patrons.

"I think that's it. You're a lifesaver, Heather. I knew
I should have taken that class with you on drawing cartoon figures, instead of a second semester of the nude
male form. But what can I say, I was weak."

"Don't worry," Heather replied. "That will come in

handy when we get a job painting the men's dressing room in a health club."

"Yeah, think of the possibilities," Abby said. "But another problem is that I'm going to be tied up here all day. I could tell them I have to leave, and will come back tomorrow. Jim wouldn't mind, but this regional manager acts like he's running a nuclear reactor. He wants the job done right away."

Would she be all right without Abby? Looking around her cozy apartment, Heather found it hard to resurrect the foreboding that seemed to permeate every corner of the Compton House. The beautiful home seemed to be overlain with a shadow of despair, but maybe, like her mother, she had been letting her fevered imaginings get the better of her.

She briefly told Abby about the fire and Caroline Webster's move back to Boston.

"So I think I'll be fine, Abby. Michael will be there later on this afternoon, and now with Caroline gone, the acts of vandalism probably will come to an end."

"A shame about the house, though," said Abby. "Now it will probably be torn down. Are you sure it's worth your time to finish the dining room?"

"Yes."

Her voice sounded very certain even to herself. She knew it wasn't just because she felt an obligation to Caroline Webster. It was more than that. She felt a sense of obligation to the house. She had to demonstrate to anyone who saw that place from now until it was demolished what the possibilities were, that underneath the tarnish, the grime, and the despair, there was a beautiful home waiting to be revealed.

"Okay," Abby said, recognizing that this was not a time to argue. "Do you want me to call you tonight?"

"Have you got a date with Jim?"

Abby laughed. "Actually, I have."

"Don't bother, then. I'll talk to you tomorrow. And don't let those shakes get you down."

"Don't worry. By the time I get done here the customers will expect their food to talk."

When Heather got back to the Compton House, it was mid-afternoon and the day had gotten warm. More like late May than late April, she thought, unpacking her gear. She walked around to the back of the house hoping to see Jack and get some help bringing her ladder back inside. But no one was visible, and there were no sounds coming from the direction of the gardens. The front door of the house was unlocked as always, and no one appeared to be around. Concluding that she was on her own, Heather brought in the paint and stencil materials first, then, leaving the front door open, she carried in the ladder, resting once or twice on the way.

In the dining room she opened up the ladder along the outside wall. She looked around with satisfaction as the afternoon sun bathed the room with light. This time there were no ugly graffiti or signs of damage. This was the way the room should always be, a happy, restful place and not the scene of childish nightmares.

Heather slid the ladder down to the front corner. Climbing up to the molding line, she came down half an inch and drew a straight line several feet in length. Then she carefully measured down the width of the stencil and drew another line. This would make the stenciling straight no matter how crooked the molding had become over the years.

After carefully taping the first length of stencil in place between the lines, she came down and opened the can of red paint for the rose blossoms. She poured some paint into a small aluminum tray. Once back up at the top of the ladder, she dipped the small round brush in the red paint. It came out a deep, rich red. She brushed off the excess on a piece of cardboard, then began to apply the paint to the first cutout of a rose using a light circular motion.

There were three roses to every foot, so she was able to move along rather quickly, and frequently had to come down the ladder and go back up again. All this up and down, plus the fact that it was hot near the ceiling, soon had her sweating. Even opening the windows at either end of the room, didn't help very much. She pulled her denim shirt out of her painter's pants and tied it up to leave her midriff exposed for coolness.

Should have worn short sleeves and a T-shirt, she thought, wiping the perspiration from her forehead on her sleeve. A sweat band wouldn't have hurt either. She was stretching forward trying to reach the last rose when someone spoke.

"You know, you remind me of something."

She carefully finished the rose before looking down at Michael. He was struggling to keep a smile from his face.

"What?" she asked, suppressing a grin of her own.

"A barmaid in one of Hogarth's orgy scenes."

Heather put on a severe frown. "Diana to a barmaid in less than a week. That must be some kind of a record for disillusionment."

"I'm not disillusioned. I'm amazed at how different you appear every time I see you."

"It's in the eyes of the beholder," Heather said, coming down the ladder.

"Then you inspire me to perceive the world differently every time I see you."

"That's because you have the artist's eye, just like my mother. You don't see the thing that's really there; you see what the thing makes you think of. I just stimulate your mind."

"I won't deny that," he said, giving her an appraising look. "Would you have it any other way?"

"How did your meeting go?" Heather asked in order to avoid his question.

"Super. It couldn't have gone better."

There was a hesitant knock at the door leading from the kitchen to the dining room. It opened and Mrs. Maxwell entered. She was carrying a tray with a bottle of champagne and two glasses.

"Thanks, Mrs. Maxwell, I'll take it," Michael said, realizing there was no table in the room. She nodded and handed him the tray. He brought it over to the ladder and carefully balanced it on a step. He poured the champagne into the glasses and offered one to Heather.

"What are we celebrating?" she asked.

"You are now looking at the new assistant director of the Massachusetts Museum of Contemporary Art."

"Congratulations!"

She clinked her glass with his, then, after a sip from the glass, she leaned forward and gave him a kiss. The taste of champagne was still on his lips. She kissed him again.

"That museum just opened, didn't it?"

"Last year. And they're looking for somebody who wants to try new things and give young artists opportunities to exhibit."

"Sounds wonderful," said Heather, grinning at the expression of boyish enthusiasm on his face.

"And best of all, I'll be free of Boston."

"Are you sure Renata won't find you out there?" Heather asked.

"It doesn't matter if she does. I told the director everything that had happened with Renata."

"What did he say?"

"He laughed and said that some day he'd tell me some of his experiences with artists. He pointed out that displaying the work of living artists is much more hazardous to your health than exhibiting the work of those long dead. I think he's looking forward to Renata's inevitable visit."

"Everything sounds great, then," Heather said.

"Oh, it gets even better than that," said Michael, taking her by the arm and leading her to the center of the dining room, from where she could see down to the great central hall of the house. "How would you like to have the opportunity to redecorate all of this?"

"What do you mean?" Heather asked, feeling her chest tighten.

"Well, the museum is only about forty miles away from here. Even using the back roads I can make the trip in an hour. I'm going to live here."

"But I thought you weren't interested in the Compton House." Heather heard a querulous note slip into her voice.

Michael's smile faded into puzzlement. "I thought you'd be pleased. I know you've been wanting to have the opportunity to work on the place, and how worried you were about its being torn down. And I guess the truth of it is that in the few days I've been here and watched what you've done with this room, some of the romance of the place has started to get to me as well."

"I didn't think you could afford what it will cost to fix the house up."

"Of course, it won't happen very quickly. We'll have to make do with the antiquated heating plant for a while, and the plumbing can't be replaced right away. We'll just take it one room at a time and see what happens." He stared at her, then shook his head. "I guess I was wrong about this. Maybe about everything. I thought you'd be thrilled."

"I guess I just feel so sorry for Caroline. I don't like gaining from another person's loss."

Michael's face hardened. "You don't think I'd take the house away from her, do you?"

Heather was silent.

"Do you think I'm somehow responsible for that fire last night?"

"No. Not really." Heather flushed, knowing that all of her suspicions were revealed on her face.

Michael turned away and carefully put his glass of champagne on the windowsill.

"Just for your information, as soon as I inherit, I plan to see to it that Caroline and I own the Compton House jointly," he said in a controlled voice. "I'm surprised that you would think that I would do it any differently."

"I guess I didn't think about it."

"I can see that. Even Jack and Mrs. Maxwell didn't accuse me of being a thief when I told them my plans."

The hurt expression on his face made Heather want to run to him and say how sorry she was.

"I'll be going out to dinner. Please feel free to spend the night," Michael said. He turned before she could reply and left the room.

Heather watched him leave. She would never have openly accused him of stealing the house from his sister, but who else could it be? Her heart told her that it couldn't be Michael, but her mind told her that there was no one else. Could she, even now, look him in the face and with all honesty tell him that she no longer suspected him? Could he really expect her to accept him on faith when their relationship had only lasted four days? And now that relationship was clearly over.

She would stay tonight. She would rehearse what she was going to say. When he was calmer and had gotten over the shock, he might be willing to listen to her explanation. He was more disappointed that she hadn't shared his enthusiasm for their fixing up the house together than angry at her suspicions.

Heather told herself all of this as she automatically opened the can of green paint and climbed the ladder to put in the rose vines. Her hand was steady and the color was perfect, but she found it hard to judge her own work through the tears.

## Chapter Thirteen

Even a long bath after she had finished painting for the day failed to relax Heather. Her mind continued to race as she tried to formulate arguments, justifications, and excuses for what had happened. She imagined in detail the expressions on Michael's face as she tried out each of her explanations on him. None of the expressions were as kind and as loving as what she had seen before she had virtually accused him of stealing from his sister. He might become less angry, but in none of her pictured scenarios could she see him completely forgiving her and having things return to the way they were.

Thoroughly miserable, she went downstairs to the front parlor where Mrs. Maxwell had promised to serve her a late dinner. The cook was in the process of setting up the table when Heather entered the room.

"How are you this evening, Mrs. Maxwell?" Heather

asked, longing for a little conversation to help raise her mood.

"Very well, thank you," Mrs. Maxwell replied, not turning her attention away from the white tablecloth she was spreading over the beautiful end table.

"There certainly are some nice things in this house," Heather said, refusing to give up.

"There used to be more," the cook said. "Mr. Leo sold off a number of items in the last year. He said he needed money."

"What a shame! They should have stayed in the family."

Mrs. Maxwell turned and gave Heather a long look. "Mr. Leo didn't care much about the family as far as I can see, or he'd never have come up with that foolish plan for inheriting the house."

"Well, at least now it looks like a Compton will inherit and the house won't be sold."

"That's what Mr. Michael tells us. I hope it's true."

"You don't think he plans to sell it after three months, do you?"

Mrs. Maxwell carefully placed the food on the table before turning to answer.

"I wouldn't know about that, miss. But he still has to live here for the three months in order to inherit."

"You don't think the vandalism has stopped?" Heather asked.

The woman shrugged. "Why should it? If somebody in town wants the Comptons out of here, he isn't going to be satisfied until every Compton has left."

After Mrs. Maxwell left the room with a warning to eat the food while it was hot, Heather sat slumped on the sofa. The woman was right, she thought, I've been so focused on the idea that Michael might have driven

Caroline away that I've ignored the fact that someone else committed the earlier acts of vandalism. Why should that person stop just because Caroline has left? That means that Michael is now the target.

Heather sat down at the table. The wonderfully aromatic stew filling the bowl in front of her had little appeal, given her state of mind. "No point in starving yourself to solve a problem," Heather recalled her occasionally practical mother saying. Smiling a little at her mother's admonition, Heather grudgingly tore off a piece of the crusty French bread in the basket next to her bowl and picked up her spoon. A few minutes later she was surprised to see that the bowl was almost empty. She lifted the napkin from the dessert plate and saw a thick slice of apple pie.

"Looks almost good enough to eat," said Jack.

Heather jumped in surprise.

"Sorry, I didn't mean to startle you," he said, briefly putting a hand on her shoulder. "I was back at the stable when I realized how chilly it had gotten after sunset. I thought you might like to have a fire."

"Thanks. That would be very nice."

Jack knelt down on one knee in front of the fireplace. She watched him begin to carefully lay the fire.

"You put in a lot of time on the job," she said.

He turned sideways to face her and nodded. "That's the drawback to living where you work. You're always on duty. Just like being on board a ship, as my Dad used to say."

"Was your father in the navy?"

"No, but I think he would like to have been." Jack paused as if trying to remember the past. "He does a lot of sailing."

"Does your family live around here?"

He shook his head. "I'm from out west."

"I guess you'll be able to keep living on the premises if Michael takes over."

"I suppose," Jack said, turning back to watch the sparks start among the kindling.

"Mrs. Maxwell seems to think that whoever has been playing tricks on us might not stop just because Caroline Webster is gone. He or she might try to drive out Michael as well."

"Hard to tell," Jack said, going over to the wood bin in the corner to select some larger pieces to add to the fire. "Michael doesn't strike me as someone who'll be easily scared off once he makes up his mind."

"That might just make the person more desperate."

Jack straightened and leaned an elbow on the mantle. The shadows from the fire played over his face, making him look older and more mysterious.

"But he's got more of a motivation to stay than just the house, doesn't he?" Jack asked.

"What do you mean?" She held her breath. Did even Jack recognize that Michael wanted the house for her sake? Did even Jack suspect that Michael had frightened away his own sister?

Jack smiled as if he read her mind but wasn't going to give her the satisfaction of admitting it.

"Well, he's going to be working pretty close by, isn't he? Caroline's from Boston, that's where her husband lives and where all her friends are. It was a crazy idea for her to want to move out here. But it makes a lot more sense for Michael."

"That's true," said Heather, starting to breathe again.

"The fire should be okay. You can throw on a couple of medium-sized logs from the bin in a few more minutes."

Heather nodded.

"Don't worry about staying upstairs alone. Mrs. Maxwell is right off the kitchen. And Michael will be back soon. Remember, he has to spend six hours a night here in order to inherit."

Suddenly looking young again, Jack gave her an awkward wave and disappeared into the hall.

After finishing her pie and having a cup of tea, Heather put a couple of logs on the fire, then went over to the love seat and curled up. She pulled the afghan over her legs even though she was wearing slacks. The chill wasn't in her body as much as in her mind. The door from the parlor to the front hall stood open, so she would be sure to hear Michael when he returned. Heather picked up the book on nineteenth century design that she had begun the other night and started to read. An hour later her head dropped to her chest and she drifted off into a sound sleep.

The chiming of the clock on the mantle woke her with a start. Eleven o'clock, she thought, staring bleary-eyed at the hands. I've been asleep for over an hour and a half. Did Michael slip into the house while I was asleep? Would he really not bother to come into the parlor to see if I was waiting up for him?

Heather stood up, shook off the stiffness in her limbs, then went out to the front hall. She opened the front door and looked down the circular drive. Michael's car wasn't there. Thinking that he could possibly have pulled it around back, Heather walked to the side of the house and looked up the side driveway. No car there either. She stood there hugging herself against the cool night breeze. Where could he be? He did have an hour before curfew, so to speak, but how close would he dare to cut it? She didn't know how Lloyd kept track of whether the Comptons were actually living in the house, but she had a feeling that he wasn't remiss in his responsibilities.

Just to be certain that Michael hadn't come home and parked his car in some remote spot, Heather went upstairs and knocked on his bedroom door. When there was no answer, she opened it and went inside. His room ran along the back of the house and was even larger than hers. Although equally depressing, it had more furniture, including two dark mahogany dressers and three large upholstered chairs. One of the chairs was next to the twin of the end table in the front parlor. With horror, Heather saw that a teacup had been tipped over out of its saucer and amber liquid had pooled on the gorgeous table top. Pulling tissues from her pocket, she attempted to wipe up the spill, but some of the brown finish came up as she wiped.

It isn't like Michael to do something like that, Heather thought. Anyone who appreciates beautiful things wouldn't carelessly damage a valuable antique.

By the time she returned to the front parlor, the clock had struck the quarter hour. Where was he? she wondered nervously. Her nap had only served to focus her mind more on what Mrs. Maxwell had said about Michael being the new target of the vandal. Could something have happened to him? The spilled tea was odd, but Heather couldn't quite imagine an irate neighbor coming into the house and kidnapping Michael from his own bedroom.

Perhaps he's having a good time at a restaurant somewhere, and has simply lost track of the time. Or perhaps he's staying out as late as he can simply to avoid talking to me.

*What if he lost the house because he was trying to avoid me?* The idea was silly, Heather knew, but feeling guilty all the same she went down the hall to the kitchen. Mrs. Maxwell's door was shut. Heather knocked twice without response.

"Were you looking for me, miss?" Mrs. Maxwell was standing behind her.

Heather spun around.

"Oh, you surprised me."

"I'm sorry. I was just checking the windows before preparing for bed."

"Mr. Compton hasn't come home yet, and I was wondering if you knew where he went for dinner."

The cook furrowed her brow. "I don't think he mentioned where he was going to me."

"It's just that it's getting rather late, given the amount of time he has to spend in the house."

Mrs. Maxwell smiled. "I wouldn't worry myself about that. I'm sure he's well aware of the time."

"I suppose," Heather said doubtfully.

"Would you like some cocoa or anything else to eat?"

"No, no thank you," Heather replied.

Wishing the cook a good night, Heather started to return to the parlor. Instead she opened the front door. Her van was still the only vehicle parked in the circle. Deciding that sitting around waiting was too much for her nerves, Heather ran back to her room, grabbed her keys, and came back down to the front foyer. She unlocked the front door and went outside. But what if Mrs. Maxwell locked the door while she was out? she thought. She didn't have a key to the outside doors. Heather raced down the hall to the dining room and unlocked one of the back windows. She could always climb in that way in an emergency.

Heather was driving out through the front gate when the reality hit her that she had absolutely no idea where to go to look for Michael. He could have gone anywhere for dinner. But doing something had to be better than sitting around doing nothing, so she turned right, knowing from the map that that was the way to the town of Compton. Whether it even had a restaurant remained to be seen.

She had traveled about two miles toward Compton when her headlights caught a car pulled over by the side of the road heading the other way. It was pulled under a low hanging tree with only part of the side clearly visible to the road. Something about it looked familiar. She slammed on the brakes and did a quick U-turn. As she pulled up behind the car, Heather was certain that it was Michael's. Leaving her headlights on she walked up to the driver's side and knocked on the window. There was no response. She peered through the driver's window. Someone was behind the wheel. Holding her breath, Heather pulled on the door handle. The dome light revealed Michael sitting slumped over in the seat. The smell of alcohol was overwhelming.

Heather reached in and shook him. Aside from a brief moan, there was no response.

"Michael, you have to get back home. You only have twenty minutes," she shouted.

His breathing remained deep and undisturbed. I can shout all night and it won't make any difference, Heather thought, there's no way he's going anywhere under his own power. In the back of her mind she wondered if he had gotten drunk because of their argument. That seemed rather childish on his part, but made her feel responsible nonetheless.

She rushed back to the van and carefully pulled it up as close as she could next to Michael's car. By getting her shoulder under his chest she was able to prop him up against the side of her van. The front seat was far too high for her to lift him, so she slid open the side doors on the van and, being careful to support his head, she gently eased him in stages into the cargo area.

Torn between driving slowly to avoid unnecessary bouncing and yet anxious to get Michael back to the Compton House within the next fifteen minutes, Heather made the return trip at a moderate pace and arrived back with seven minutes to spare. Leaving Michael in the back of the van, she tried the front door. As she had feared, it was locked. Her first impulse was to ring the bell and alert Mrs. Maxwell. Heather had never seen any-one completely unconscious from alcohol before, and she wondered if Michael's condition was life threaten-ing. But just as her finger was about to reach the button, she realized that Michael would probably not want the cook to see him in this condition. Perhaps it would be wiser to get him inside and see if his condition improved within the next couple of hours.

The immediate problem was to get the front door opened and to get Michael inside. She knew she could never carry him up the stairs to his bedroom, but she might be able to partially carry him as far as the front parlor. At least he could sleep in a chair next to the fire instead of on the hard metal floor of a cold van.

Heather went around to the back of the house, being careful not to trip in the darkness. Always having lived in built-up areas, she had never realized that the true darkness of the country was like having a piece of black velvet in front of your face. Feeling her way along the wall, she finally found the window she had left ajar. She pushed the window open to give herself enough room to climb inside. Just as she was about to hoist her leg over the sill a hand came down on her shoulder.

"What's going on here?" a harsh voice asked.

"Who's that?" Heather asked, automatically trying to shrug off the hand, but it grasped her tighter.

"Is that you Heather?"

"Jack?" she turned to face him.

"Heather, what are you doing out here?"

"Mrs. Maxwell's locked me out. I left a window open so I could get back inside." She knew that abbreviated version didn't make much sense. Mercifully, Jack didn't ask any questions.

"Let me give you a hand," he said, climbing through the window with two easy strides. He then reached out and easily pulled Heather through the opening. "Now let's go down to the parlor and sort this out."

By the time they reached the front parlor and turned on the lights, Heather knew that she had to tell Jack the truth. Her wandering around had to be explained, and with Jack's help she was sure they could get Michael up to his bedroom.

She sat in a wing chair by the fire which was little more than a deep reddish glow by now. Jack stood by the fireplace and looked down at her with a quizzical expression.

"When it got late and Michael still hadn't returned, I began to get worried. So I took the van and went out looking for him."

Jack nodded, his eyes not leaving her face.

"I found him unconscious in his car about two miles from here off to the side of the road."

Jack looked at his watch. "We'd better go get him. Although it's already after eleven, so technically it's too late. But maybe Lloyd won't find out."

"Oh, I brought him back with me before eleven. He's

out in my van. Since he's on the property, I think it's okay."

"I'm surprised you could lift him," Jack said, leaning on the mantle and staring at her.

"Well, I can't carry him up to his bedroom alone. And I was hoping that you would help me."

"I'll do better than that. I'll carry him up to his room myself. I'll even stay with him until he sobers up."

"Thanks, but I'll give you a hand. And I'd like to stay with him in case he needs a doctor."

"A doctor for a hangover. I don't think he'll need that," Jack said with a bark of laughter.

"Nevertheless . . ."

"Okay, look, you can help me carry him upstairs, then get some sleep. I'll stay with him, and if he doesn't seem right, I'll wake you and we can get a doctor."

Heather smiled her gratitude. "Thanks. That's a great idea."

They went out in the front foyer and Jack began to unlock the door.

"I'm surprised you were able to spot his car pulled under a tree like that," he said.

Heather's breath caught in her chest.

"How did you know his car was under a tree?" she asked.

"You just told me," Jack said easily.

"No I didn't. I just said it had been a couple of miles down the road."

Jack turned back to the door and re-locked it.

"You parked Michael's car under that tree," Heather said, backing away from him.

"And nobody was going to get hurt. It was a perfect plan. If only you hadn't run out looking for him like a lovesick little fool."

Jack's face twisted in anger and frustration. In the dim light of the hall, the image her mind had been searching for slipped into place and stayed. The face in the picture.

"You're Alex Compton!"

"Not likely. He'd be in his sixties if he were alive. But he was my father. I'm Andrew."

"But you died with your father in a boating accident."

"Apparently not," he said, as a slow smile curved his face. "It was just useful that I appear to be dead for a while."

"In order to get the Compton House?"

"Of course."

"Does it mean that much to you?"

"What I can get for selling it means that much. There was a guy around the other day offering a couple of million. And there will be others with even better offers."

"And you've been living on the grounds."

"That's right, six months with miserable old Uncle Leo, who was so blind that he never came close to recognizing me. When he finally kicked off, all I had to do was stay here for three more months and get rid of dear cousins Caroline and Michael. Then I'd reveal who I was and become the sole owner."

"So there never was anyone in town trying to scare the Comptons away?" Heather asked.

"I made the whole story up. Pretty creative, I thought. Actually I got the idea from Lloyd, he's the one who thought some of the townspeople might still hate the family."

Heather took a step away from him.

"What are you going to do now?"

"First I'm going to dump cousin Michael back in his car."

"How did you get him there in the first place?"

"Drugged his tea. After that I kept him in the stable for about four hours until it got dark. I poured some liquor over him. Then I took off down the road, parked the car, shoved him behind the wheel, and walked back. I figured he wouldn't be found until after midnight. No one would be real sympathetic if he lost the house because he got so drunk he couldn't find his way home. Even he wouldn't be sure it hadn't happened that way. Guess it was my bad luck that you decided to go searching for him."

He took a step towards her. "But I've got to make sure you don't go anywhere while I'm making my little trip."

Heather turned and ran across the foyer and down the hall to the kitchen. She could hear Jack's heavy footsteps behind her as she plowed through the kitchen door. Mrs. Maxwell's door was closed, but Heather burst through it without knocking. The cook was sitting in a chair knitting.

"Mrs. Maxwell, Jack is actually Andrew Compton and he's trying to take the house away from Michael," Heather said, then paused to catch her breath.

The cook slowly rose from her chair and placed the knitting in a basket at her feet. Then she walked over to Heather and slapped her hard across the face.

Spun round by the force of the blow, Heather saw Jack standing in the doorway with a triumphant smile on his face.

"I see you've met my mother," he said.

## Chapter Fourteen

Heather sat in the hard wooden chair into which Jack had forced her. She was by the kitchen table with Jack standing only an arm's reach away. His mother stood by the sink and stared at her. Heather's cheek burned from where the woman had slapped her.

"You're Alex Compton's wife?" Heather asked.

"Denise Compton, his widow," the woman spat out the words as if her relationship with her husband was something she'd rather forget.

"Why did you come out here to work for Leo Compton?"

Asking questions as though they were having a friendly chat over coffee around the kitchen table seemed surrealistic; but Heather instinctively felt that the more time she got them to the spend answering questions, the further she delayed their decision as to what to do with her.

At first Denise Compton just stared, and Heather's heart sank at the thought that the woman would refuse to answer, but then she shrugged as if answering questions now didn't matter.

"We all knew about Leo's will. He notified us five years ago of what we would have to do to inherit the house. Alex talked all the time about moving back out here when Leo died and trying to get his share of it. He was one of the brothers, after all. He said that meant he deserved a part of the place more than Caroline or Michael."

"But then he died in a boating accident," said Heather. A sudden thought came to her. "He did die, didn't he?"

"He died all right, and none too soon," said the woman with a bitter laugh. "He'd run through all the money his father had given him years before he met me and never did adjust to having to work for a living. All he wanted to do was take out that small sailboat of his and spend his time at the yacht club talking with those who were still rich. He mostly left me to earn the money working in restaurant kitchens. Once Leo died, he promised, he'd pay me back in spades for all my hard work."

"Why did you pretend that Jack—I mean Andrew—was dead?" Heather asked.

The woman gave her a shrewd look. "I knew that the only way Andrew and I were going to get rich was to get the house and grounds all to ourselves. The way to do that was to let Michael and Caroline think they were the only ones left to inherit. After Leo died, Andrew and I would scare them off, and then Andrew would be the sole heir to meet the terms of the will. I got the job working as a cook for Leo, so we'd be ready when the time came. In the three years I worked here, Leo had lots of good offers for the property, so I knew it was worth the wait."

"But that could have taken forever." Heather paused. "You didn't . . ." She stopped, not wanting to ask the question.

"Kill him?" Denise Compton finished it for her with a smile. "I thought about it often enough. He was a miserable old man and frail enough that many times I was tempted to give him a shove down the stairs and end all the waiting. But I didn't want anyone to suspect foul play. I might have done it anyway if he had gone on much longer, but then his heart gave out."

"And you got Andrew the job so he'd be living on the grounds and qualify to inherit."

She nodded. "As soon as Leo really started to fail, I got Andrew the job and a place to live in the stables. I pretended he was a boy I'd met in town who would work cheap for money to go to school. Leo always liked anyone who would work cheap. After Leo died, all we had to do was keep Andrew on the property for three months and drive out the other Comptons."

"It was you and Andrew that I heard talking the day after Anna was attacked."

"Andrew didn't like my scaring her off like that. Thought she was cute." The woman looked at her son with contempt. "She was just in the way, always hanging around in the kitchen all the time. Sooner or later she'd have seen something she shouldn't. I just gave her a hard shove. Didn't do her any harm."

"Which one of you left me in the well?" Heather asked.

She saw Andrew shuffle his feet.

"I saw you down there," Andrew admitted. "I wanted to get you out, but Mom said that you'd gotten yourself into trouble with all your snooping. So it served you right."

Denise Compton stared at Heather. "I knew you were going to be a problem from the first. And when you started snooping around those paintings, I was sure of it. Leo had left the one of himself and his brothers in the hall. As soon as he died, I took it down and stored it with the others in the attic. No sense running the risk that anyone would spot a family resemblance between Alex and Andrew."

"My mother painted that picture," Heather said dully.

"A good likeness of my late husband," the woman said, then she frowned. "It would have been better if no one had saved you from that well. Now we have to decide what to do with you."

"Why not let me go? You haven't done anything really wrong," Heather said quickly. "Even if it could be proven that you were behind the vandalism, what you've done has mostly been minor. Michael and Caroline would probably not prosecute in order to keep the whole thing out of the papers. And Andrew could still claim his share of the house, if he lives over the stable for six more weeks."

The woman shook her head. "If we stop now, Andrew will have to divide what we get for the house with Michael. For three long years I worked like a slave for that old man. I've earned the entire thing."

"What should we do now, Mom?" asked Andrew.

Nervousness was clear in his voice. He had gone from the self-assured bully he'd been out in the hall to an uncertain, worried boy. In a moment of insight Heather saw that Andrew, like his father, wasn't evil. He was weak and ineffectual, a ready tool for someone like Denise Compton. That was what her mother had seen and hated in Alex, Heather realized. Not evil, but a person easily seduced by evil. That was why he always seemed so shadowy in the painting. He lacked any real character or substance of his own.

"We'll tie her up," said the woman. "Then we'll take her and Michael back to where his car is. We'll put them both in the car and take it out to that hairpin curve where the cliff drops off. That's sort of a lovers' lane, but no one will be out there this late. Then we'll push the car over the cliff."

Andrew shook his head doubtfully.

"That's murder, Mom. The police are going to look into that."

The woman thought some more. "I'll say that Michael came home drunk and had a fight with Heather. When he went back out to the car she insisted on going with him because he was too drunk to drive. The police will think they went out there to make up and Michael was too drunk to notice when the car started to roll."

"But if they find Heather all tied up . . ." Andrew began.

Denise Compton looked at Heather as if she weren't even there. "We'll untie her at the last minute. If she puts up a fight, we'll hit her on the head. The police will think it happened in the fall."

"You'll be caught. You won't get away with this," Heather shouted, aware even through her fear that she was mouthing the cliches she'd heard in every bad police show she'd ever seen.

"We'll take our chances," the woman said. She motioned to her son, who grabbed Heather by the arm and jerked her to her feet. He began to drag her toward the door.

"I'd stop right there if I were you." Lloyd stood in the

doorway, a double-barreled shotgun aimed in their direction.

Everyone was silent for a long moment.

"Andrew, take that gun away from him," Denise Compton said. "He's an old man."

"Don't do anything foolish, boy," Lloyd said, not taking his eyes off Andrew. "I've already called the state police on my cell phone. So the game is over."

"Let us go, Lloyd," Denise said, instantly switching into a wheedling tone. "We haven't done anything really bad. We'll just go away and not come back."

The old man shook his head. "I think what I just heard would be called conspiracy to commit murder. I don't know much law, but that sounds pretty serious to me."

"Is that the old shotgun from the stables?" Andrew asked, starting to rise up on the balls of his feet.

"Yep."

"Why that thing's been covered with rust for so long and the shells are so old that you'll probably kill yourself if you pull the trigger."

Lloyd grinned and slowly drew back the hammers. "I worried about that myself, boy. That's why I cleaned it today and bought some new ammo."

"You'll kill Heather, too, if you shoot," said Denise.

A worried expression passed over Lloyd's face. As Heather felt Andrew's grip begin to tighten on her arm, she pulled away from him and ran to stand next Lloyd.

"Looks like that's one problem solved," Lloyd said. "Now if you'd like to see if this gun still works, you're welcome to find out."

Andrew glanced at his mother. Seeing nothing more than a defeated expression, he took a step back and leaned against the table.

"That's fine," Lloyd said, smiling. "That's just fine."

## Chapter Fifteen

The next morning Michael awakened with the worst headache he'd ever experienced in his life. When he'd come downstairs and found Heather in the kitchen making coffee and preparing pancake batter, he'd asked where Mrs. Maxwell was.

"You might want a cup of coffee first," Heather warned.

He'd started to protest, but the expression on her face and the pain that extended from the back of his neck to behind his eyes made him slump silently into a chair. After he finished his first cup of coffee and began reluctantly to eat a pancake, Heather described the events of last evening for him.

"So Lloyd held them until the police arrived?" he asked, starting to shake his head in amazement then thinking better of it.

"Yes. Apparently he's been keeping a very close eye

on the house since all this trouble started. He wasn't only making sure that you and Caroline kept to the rules, he was also trying to catch the vandal."

"I never would have thought he had it in him."

"Lloyd is a man of hidden talents," Heather said with a mischievous smile. "He recognized right away that I was like your grandmother Sarah."

"Oh, and how's that?"

"He saw right away that Sarah and I shared the same love for this house and had a vision of what it should look like."

Michael reached over and squeezed her hand. "I saw that too. And in my own clumsy way that's what I was trying to tell you yesterday. I want you to make this house into that vision. I know I came on too strong and made it sound as if I wanted to give you the house in order to bribe you into staying here. That isn't what I meant at all. What I was trying to say is that, as we fix up this house together, maybe we'll both discover that it really was meant to be ours, yours and mine."

Heather leaned forward and gently kissed him on the lips. He tried to press harder, but she backed away.

"I want you to know that I didn't really think you started that fire the other night. I let my head overrule my heart. I thought it had to be a Compton and you were the only candidate."

Michael nodded. "I hadn't thought it through the way you had. But later, as I was sitting up in my room drinking the tea that Mrs. Maxwell had brought me, I started to see why you suspected me. Since I knew that I wasn't the culprit, I started to think about who else it could be. Jack was the only newcomer to the house who could possibly be a Compton. I had never thought about how we even look a bit alike. I was about to come down and apologize to you and suggest that we look into Jack's background, when I passed out."

This time when he pressed his lips hard against hers Heather didn't resist. Her hands gently went behind his head and pressed him closer to her.

The doorbell rang twice before they separated.

"Since all the servants have fled, sir, I'll get the door," said Heather, dropping a quick curtsey.

When Heather opened the door, Renata Sisco stood there wearing a demure little sundress that still managed to accentuate her beautiful arms and shoulders.

"Is Michael Compton here?" she asked coolly, quickly concealing her surprise at Heather's answering the door.

"I'll check." As Heather began to turn she realized that Michael was standing behind her.

"Hello, Renata," he said.

"Michael, I'd like to talk with you."

"Yes," Michael said, not moving.

"It's rather personal."

"Whatever you have to say, you can say right here."

Awareness flashed over Renata's face.

"I see." She paused, unsure whether to continue. "I heard about your new job yesterday when I was at the museum. Congratulations."

"Thank you."

She straightened her shoulders. "I wanted to tell you that I said some things the other day that I didn't mean, as I'm sure you did as well. I wanted to apologize. And I thought that perhaps we could let bygones be bygones and start over."

"Thank you for the apology, Renata. But I meant what I said the other day." Michael hesitated for a moment, as if searching for something else to say, then went on, "Good-bye, Renata, and good luck."

Renata stared at Michael as if she couldn't understand what he meant, and she only turned away as Heather gently but firmly closed the door.

"You're almost done with the first floor. Not bad," said Abby, walking along next to Heather as they toured the first floor of the Compton House.

Heather smiled. "What do you mean 'not bad'?" We've done a great job."

"You've done the great job. Okay, I've been living here with you and Michael for the last three months since you got rid of Denise Compton and her evil son Andrew, but I've been doing other jobs so much of the time that we've hardly had time to talk. This has been your project."

Heather nodded. Even since a local paper had covered the story of what had happened at the Compton House, Passionate Painters had been besieged with business. They were even thinking about taking on their first male employee now that Jimmy had quit the Burger Hut.

"It's been my project and Michael's and even Caroline's."

"Yeah. It was really decent of George Webster to offer to fund the restoration."

"Well, Michael and I have agreed that Caroline will always be half owner of the house even though she's decided not to live here. Her therapist thinks that occasional visits to the family home might be beneficial as a way of recovering from the loss of her parents."

"I guess her first visit will be in about six weeks, right?"

"When she'll be standing next to you in my wedding party."

Abby frowned. "I hope you didn't let her pick the

color we're going to wear. Dark green makes me look big as a whale."

"My mother is helping me with the color choices."

"How's she doing with this whole thing?"

"Amazingly well. She's happy that if I'm not going to be an artist, at least I'm marrying a man who appreciates art. And she wasn't the least bit surprised when it turned out that there were several outstanding warrants in Alaska for Denise and Andrew on charges of fraud and embezzlement. It sort of confirmed her original view of Alex."

"Your mother doesn't give up," Abby said, grinning.

"Let's say she doesn't change her mind easily."

"This wedding will be quite an event. Michael was telling me that you've invited the entire town of Compton."

"It seemed like a good start in making amends for all the resentment between the townspeople and the Comptons that's built up over the generations. But it's only a beginning. I'm hoping that Michael and I can take part in revitalizing the area, maybe by selling the parcel of property farthest from the house and using the proceeds to set up a community center."

They walked out the front door and stood on the step for a moment.

"Do you remember how this house gave you the creeps when you first saw it?" Abby asked.

Heather raised her head to take in the entire front facade. "A house does have an atmosphere, but it isn't something that's in the wood or the bricks or the mortar. It comes from the lives that are lived there. If a house is old enough, some of those lives are bound to have been unhappy, desperate, or filled with despair; but that doesn't stop those of us who are living from making it a happier place by filling it with laughter, love, and light."

Abby reached over and impetuously gave her friend a hug. Heather was surprised to see tears in Abby's eyes.

"What's the matter?" she asked.

"Nothing," Abby said, brushing the tears away with the back of her hand. "I guess I'm just getting soft since Jimmy and I have been talking about the future. Maybe all this nonsense about building a home is starting to make sense. Either that or I've been inhaling too many paint fumes."

Michael's car pulled around the circle and Abby headed for her van.

"I'd better get going so you and Michael can 'ooh' and 'ahh' about the house some more. You're as bad as a couple with a new baby. 'Course, once you have a baby that will put a stop to improving the house."

"We'll see," Heather said serenely. "Maybe that's just an improvement of a different kind."

Abby waved to Michael as she drove past him around the drive. He pulled Heather into his arms and gave her a long kiss.

"I came home to take my beautiful wife-to-be out to lunch," he announced.

"How lovely, but won't they miss you at work?"

"My first exhibit is up; we have to return tonight for the opening reception. Until then, we're free as two birds."

"I'm sorry, but there's a faux-marbling technique that I really wanted to try on the downstairs bathroom this afternoon."

Michael's face clouded, then he laughed, as he saw the glint of humor in her eyes.

"Come away with me, my sweet, I have a picnic basket in the trunk and I know a little bower where no one will disturb us."

Heather was about to speak when Michael put a finger to her lips.

"You know, you remind me of something."

She pushed his finger away, laughing. "What's that?"

"You remind me of Aphrodite, the goddess of love."

Heather gently took his hand and held it in her own.

"May it always be so, darling, may it always be so."